THE FIRST TIME THAT
VICTORIA SAW STEVE KAPTAIN,
HE WAS IN BED
AND A KNIFE WAS IN HER HAND

But Victoria swiftly learned how impotent her knife
was against this man's steely strength and iron will.
Always she knew that Steve Kaptain would come to
claim her, and all that she had, as his own; and he
would never doubt that it was his right to do so.
Now Victoria was no longer a fear-ravished girl. She
was a magnificent woman. Now she could use far
more than a knife as her instrument of violence and
vengeance. And now she would test once and for all
how enduring was this man's hold over her—and
how real was her will to resist . . .

SWEET GOLDEN SUN

Parris Afton Bonds

POPULAR LIBRARY • NEW YORK

Published by Popular Library, a unit of CBS
Publications, the Consumer Publishing Division of CBS Inc.

June, 1978

ISBN: 0-445-04226-5

The author gratefully acknowledges use of *Rip Ford's Texas*
edited by Stephen B. Oates and published by the
University of Texas Press, and *Robert Simpson Neighbors
and the Texas Frontier* by Kenneth Neighbors and published
by the Texana Press of Waco, as sources in the
writing of this book.

Most of the characters herein are figures out of Texas's romantic history. Although some of the events relating to these characters are fictitious and a few of the dates have been changed to retain the continuity of the story, a great part of this novel follows the true accounts of the famous Texas Ranger, Dr. Rip (John) Ford.

Prologue

✠✠✠✠✠✠✠✠✠✠

Night was quickly pulling her blanket over the dusty
pueblo of Vallejo, and the old Mexican, dressed in the
loose, white cotton *camisa* and *calzones* of the peon,
hurried through the deserted streets. As he passed the
carnicería, he came to an abrupt halt. The butcher,
Guido Azcona, swung lifelessly from the same timbers
on which he strung his beef for butchering.

The peon had seen many such horrors since the
Texas Mounted Rifles Regiment had ridden into the
village three days earlier, slaying everything in sight so
that the streets ran slippery with blood. He genuflected
and, moving carefully around the swinging form, scur-

ried on. Soon the Texas Rangers, *los Diablos Tejanos,* would ride in from one of their forages, and the atrocities would begin again.

From out of the night came that hideously screeching Texas Yell that sent the blood curdling like sour milk through the veins of every Mexican. Behind adobe walls the families hid in fear, barring their splintered wooden doors and shudders. They knew the deadly revenge those Rangers bore like a cross embedded in their savage hearts.

More than once since the company had been quartered there, the shouts of "Remember Goliad!" and "Remember the Alamo!" had echoed among the adobe buildings, and some poor unarmed "greaser" would "eat his last tortilla," as the Rangers seemed fond of saying.

Those enlisted frontiersmen—dressed in a wild assortment of clothing, bobtailed coats or long-tailed blues with black leather hats and coonskin caps—were a terrifying sight. Always coated with dust and sporting huge, grizzly beards which gave them a barbarous appearance, each Ranger carried a pair of Colt revolvers strapped to his hips, a bowie knife tucked into his belt, and the long rifle clutched in his callused hands.

That particular night the citizens were more anxious than usual. It was a holiday for the Texans, July 4th of 1846, and soon the company of Rangers would overrun the cantina and brothel, spilling out into the street in loud, boisterous merrymaking and drunken brawling.

And that particular night would leave its imprint, like the claw mark of a wild animal, on the mind and heart of Victoria Romero de Kenton's thirteen-year-old body.

8

In all truth, Victoria knew she could not blame the weak-willed Mother Superior for what happened that night.

For, indeed, the nasty looking Ranger with the tobacco-stained teeth would have torn the convent apart, room by room, as he threatened. He had come to the dank, musty cloisters seeking the cache he had been told of, and demanding further refreshment be brought to the Rangers at the cantina.

Like a lamb for the slaughter, Mother Teresa sent Victoria as emissary with the inebriating gift of propitiation, the poor-quality, convent-made wine. There was no one else Mother Teresa deemed suitable to take the girl's place. Only Victoria, the daughter of a deceased English mother and Mexican father, spoke English, in Vallejo. Her brother Pedro had already forgotten the few English words his mother had so patiently taught him.

Victoria was not a cowardly child, but neither was she foolhardy. So it was with real fear that the slim girl slipped through the wrought-iron gates of the convent orphanage that evening and started down the rutted dirt street.

"Espérame, hermana!"

Victoria turned, and relief flooded her gardenia-white complexion as she watched the mischief-loving seven-year-old brother squeeze through the gate's ornamental grille. With him to accompany her, she did not feel quite so apprehensive.

At that end of town the street was dark and deserted. But like moths driven toward light, the two children proceeded toward the brightly lit cantina at the street's far end, carrying in their arms bottles of wine the sisters had kept stored in the convent's cellar.

As they neared the swinging doors of the cantina, a mournful trumpet blared out from within. A Spanish guitar joined in the haunting, brassy ballad to produce shrill, discordant notes—as if the Mexican musicians played under sweating pressure.

Victoria hesitated there at the door, as the odor of tobacco smoke and the fumes of mescal enveloped her, but Pedro urged her on.

"Cobarde!" he hissed, giving her a playful shove at the small of her back. "Since when have you been afraid, *hermana*? They are only stupid louts, these *gringos*!"

It was then that a lardy-looking Ranger stumbled through the doors and fell in a sprawl before the two children, his beefy head dangling from the boardwalk's edge in a drunken stupor.

Both Victoria and Pedro jumped back in surprise, but Pedro edged nearer when he saw what protruded from the man's hip pocket. It was a red handkerchief, worn by most of the Rangers—and, as the Mexican sombrero was a souvenir to those fierce fighting men, so the red handkerchief was to the Mexicans.

"No, Pedrocito!" Victoria whispered hoarsely, as the boy ignoring her warning, stealthily crept nearer, his hand reaching for the prize.

"Hey! What the blasted hell's going on here?" a heavy, gritty voice demanded.

Both Victoria and Pedro looked upward to see the red-bearded giant swaying above them. Before Victoria was sure what had happened, Pedro grabbed the handkerchief and sprinted off in the darkness. The giant drew the Colt revolver in one rapid movement and fired. The small shadow pitched forward as if thrown from a bronco.

It was funny, Victoria would think much later, that all she remembered from that horrifying night was the beautiful burst of yellow fire from the pistol. For what had followed she had buried deeply within herself, knowing instinctively that to remember it would surely destroy her reasoning.

Sweaty hands tore at her clothing, and a foul-smelling mouth cursed her race even as the hairy body violated her own there on the boardwalk. Her screams were drowned out by the din of noise from within. But had it been as quiet as the cemetery, no one would have heeded her pleas.

The man grunted and buttoned his pants—as if finished with a distasteful duty. He kicked her in the stomach with a boot reeking of manure, and Victoria curled up with pain as the giant—contemptuously spitting the word "greaser!"—wandered back through the cantina's swinging doors.

Slowly Victoria began walking, only her uneven gait betraying the pain she endured. Down the darkened street she hobbled, not even halting before her brother's lifeless body. In a daze she walked the rest of that night and into the early noon hours of the next day.

When the heat and thirst became too much for her, she would pause in the scanty shade of the red-flowered nopal and put a small stone from the desert floor in her mouth. The stone caused a more abundant flow of saliva and assuaged her thirst.

She continued on, seeing neither the thorny and leafless vegetation about her nor the brassy sky and boiling sun above her, until she reached the Rio San Juan, just outside the pueblo of Santiago.

There, at the river's sandy bank, an old, bony man, bleached like parchment by the sun, was filling casks with water and loading them on his burros. As the apparition moved toward him, his weak, watery eyes grew large with fright.

It was some seconds before he recognized the blistered form, with its dust-caked rags and long, black, matted hair, as belonging to a human. The light, sapphire-colored eyes, legacy of the girl's lovely English mother, stared at the old man without seeing him, and the beautifully shaped full lips, now distorted by blisters, parted for speech, but no sound came forth.

After giving the girl water and a stale tortilla, which she devoured like a small coyote, he placed her on one of his burros and took her into Santiago, where he discharged his load.

Like Vallejo, Santiago was a poverty-stricken village, and no one there wanted an extra mouth to feed. There was nothing for the old man to do but take her on northward to his sister-in-law's place in the border town of Reynosa.

For two more days the girl traveled as if in a coma, before she was finally bathed and put to bed by the caustic and domineering proprietress of the boarding-house. At first Rose, the old man's fat sister-in-law, thought the girl's mind had snapped, for Victoria seemed to remember nothing. But under the middle-aged woman's frisky kindness the girl slowly emerged from the self-induced hypnotic state. By the end of the week Victoria had regained her former liveliness.

And by the end of the month, Rose felt she could

explain to Victoria, now a housemaid there, how the girl was brought into Reynosa by the brother-in-law. When she had finished, Rose inhaled one of the cigars she habitually smoked and waited for Victoria to tell something about herself.

The girl watched in amazement as a smoke ring drifted upward from Rose's painted mouth before she responded with the little she knew.

Reciting in a flat tone, as if she had trained herself by rote never to forget her past, she began her brief story by telling Rose she was thirteen. Which was but a guess. For she and Pedro had been brought to Vallejo's Santa Guadalupe Convent in a frightened state of confusion. But she knew that she had been with the sisters there for over six years. That Victoria was sure of.

That and the knowledge that her father had been a wealthy *hacendado* who insisted on taking his beloved English wife with him everywhere. It had been on a business trip to San Antonio that they had been ambushed by Comancheros. Not even her father's heavily armed guards had been able to defend them against the abruptness of the attack. Somewhere in the wasteland of Wild Horse Desert lay their bones, bleached by the sun and scattered by the winds.

Just as her father's hacienda and its contents had been scattered by the Mexican government. Confiscated and distributed to the local guerillas as a pacifier against their threats of terrorism.

Turned out of their home, she and Pedro, like countless other homeless children, would have literally starved on the little scraps salvaged from the leftovers of other families. But the *ama de llaves,* the Romeros'

13

devoted housekeeper, took them into Vallejo to the convent.

Not that the convent had been that much better. Victoria and Pedro had battled among the other orphans for the small mound of clothes deposited in the children's room each morning. Small for her age, Victoria often was forced to wear clothing that dragged the dusty tiled floors by several inches. And never did she have shoes. But at least they had eaten twice daily.

There was one other thing Victoria was sure of. She had known the security of wealth and the cruelty of poverty. And she knew that one way or another she would make certain she escaped the latter.

She summed up the remaining moments of her life before Rose's brother-in-law found her—of taking the wine bottles from the orphanage to the saloon, and her brother's subsequent death. But why and how and what followed, she had no recollection.

No recollection, that is, until she entered one of Rose's boarding rooms to clean it and saw the Texas Ranger.

I

❖❖❖❖❖❖❖❖❖❖❖

When first Victoria saw his long, lean body stretched out on the four-poster in exhausted sleep, she did not realize the intensity of the hatred that simmered just beneath her breast.

But the bright red handkerchief carelessly knotted beneath the spare, angular face blotted everything in the room . . . everything in her mind. And the memories of that night four years earlier came flooding over her like the high tide of the Mexican Gulf to fill the vacuum the amnesia had created.

The pain, the disgust, the blood, the shame . . . and

most of all the hate. The emotions mingled in a vortex of rage.

The rage in her heart, it seemed to Victoria, turned everything a blazing red. Yet, for all that, she was in complete control of her body, if not her mind.

Drawing the small knife she carried strapped to her right thigh for protection, she quietly closed the room's door and crossed to the sleeping form. Cautiously, she bent over the Ranger, raising the gleaming blade for the plunge. For an eternal minute the blade hung suspended in the air as Victoria relished the imminent release of long awaited revenge. True, the man before her was not grizzly-bearded as the other had been, but clean-shaven. Still, the Texas *sangrientes* were all alike. Filthy, savage beasts.

In a swift arc the knife curved downwards, only to be buried in the bed's lumpy mattress. In a lightning movement that was but a blur the man rolled from her, as lithe as the desert cat he hunted. One bronzed hand snaked out and, grasping the small-boned wrist in a steel-like grip, jerked her downward across him while the other locked about her throat.

"The devil's horns!" he cursed low and softly as his sage-green eyes in the sun-darkened face took in the enemy he had captured. With the girl's skirt hiked up about her thighs, she was all legs, reminding him of a wild colt he had once tamed.

Victoria kicked and tried to free herself from the tight embrace while his steely gaze raked her body, taut against his with the anger that infused her.

"*Déjame!*" she hissed.

Ignoring her order to be released, he tightened his

16

grip about her wrist, and the knife dropped to the floor with a thud.

"Rosie threatened to send one of her girls up here, but I didn't expect a young'n like you. My God, you're just a child!"

Victoria's spine went rigid with indignation, and she felt the iron hardness of his body against hers with a jolt of surprise. She flinched, moving as far away from him as his iron hold permitted.

"I am not a child! I was seventeen this spring." She bit her lip to still its trembling, while each separate nerve in her body quivered with her innate mistrust of all men.

If the stranger who watched her so intently was aware of this, he gave no indication. Nor did he show surprise at hearing the English on her provocatively shaped but still childish lips. Instead, the green eyes, almost lost in the forest of black lashes, were half-closed, as if he found the situation amusing.

"So Rosie's got you working here?" he asked, releasing her finally. "I didn't figure the old gal to be that corrupt."

Victoria knew what he was talking about. Rose kept several girls in the back part of the boardinghouse for the pleasure of her customers—merchants, cowhands, politicians, *vaqueros*, and whatever straggler might happen in on the gambling that went on in the room back of the kitchen. Only old Nita, the cook, and Victoria were exempted from the evening duties of the *putas*. But during the day the prostitutes cleaned the rooms and worked just as Victoria did.

"You're despicable!" Victoria said and pushed her-

17

self from the loathsome male body that smelled of wood smoke, leather, and tobacco.

But the man bounded to her side in one liquid movement, standing so far above her she had to bend her head backwards to meet the eyes that studied her.

Her knife lay lightly balanced in the long fingers that held it out to her. She looked at the knife and back at him again.

The stranger smiled, a slow half-smile that betrayed the even white teeth in the bronzed face. A powerful face with jutting cheekbones and a square jaw and a nose that was straight and high-bridged. In spite of the sun wrinkles about the penetrating green eyes, he looked younger than she had at first supposed. Maybe thirty.

But it was the long, beautifully carved lips with the deep indention in the center of the lower lip and the flared nostrils that held Victoria's attention. Despite the countenance chiseled by sun and wind and scarred by some stray arrowheads and bullets, there was the suggestion of a sensual nature.

As if the man sensed Victoria's sudden uneasiness and sought to detain her, he said, "Why did you want to kill me, little she-wolf?"

"I—I thought you were someone else." She didn't know if he believed her, but he passed the knife to her, shaft first.

"No man likes a blade at his ribs when he makes love, *corazón.*"

"It sometimes serves as a stimulant," she answered, wondering what had prompted her to make such a ribald remark.

The man threw back his head and roared with

laughter. "I'd hate to tangle with you when you're a little bit older."

He jerked one of her long black braids playfully, and the keen eyes crinkled in a smile. "Now get along, *bebé*. I've gone without sleep two days, and I'm bushed."

Victoria glared at the man frostily before spinning on her toes and crossing the room.

"Corazón!"

She whirled at the door to face him again, her long flower-patterned skirt swirling about her ankles.

He flipped a shiny gold piece across the space that separated them. With a reflexive action her hand caught the coin, the first gold piece she had seen.

"Find some other trade to ply," he said and threw himself across the bed, prepared to sleep again, already forgetting her presence.

Victoria wanted to hurl the gold piece at him. He had made her feel cheap, and she didn't like the feeling. She was suddenly glad and grateful, as she shut the door on the detestable Ranger, that Rose had spared her the lot that so often fell to young girls left to make their own way in the world.

Though, at first, in her naïvete, Victoria had resented the special status accorded the other girls who worked at Rose's, for Rose provided them with what Victoria thought was beautiful clothing and sweet, heavy perfumes.

But one day in Victoria's second year at Rose's, the grossly fat woman took her aside and said unsparingly, "Victoria, these women, *rameras* that they are, they sell their bodies to the men to be used however the worthless *chacals* want." The woman's raisin-black eyes fastened on the girl. "Do you understand me?"

Victoria had nodded, though at the time she was not sure.

"And this," Rose continued briskly, "is not what I have in mind for you, *chiquita*." The proprietress's eyes took on a far away look. "One day you'll be a great lady, and you'll invite me to your *mansión*. And I'll bounce your children on my huge lap just as if they were my own *nietos*."

"But I don't want to marry, *patrona*. Ever!"

"Bah! Of course you do. And in a few more years, when you're ripe, you'll be besieged with offers. Why, anyone has only to look at that creamy skin of yours and that fine, aquiline nose to know that you're of the Spanish aristocrats, the *gachupines*! No *mestizo* like me, with only Indians for ancestors."

And that was when Rose had given Victoria the knife, urging her to carry it with her always, for some of her customers, Rose warned, sometimes went on drunken rampages. And even Miguel, the hired guard, she reminded Victoria, couldn't be everywhere at once.

Victoria looked down at the knife she held in one hand and the gold piece she held in the other. They were just another reminder: Never again would she let herself be humbled—for her race or her sex. She would see to it that if she had nothing else, she would retain her pride.

"That one? Keep away from him, *chiquita*," Rose answered, going through the day's receipts. "Steve Kaptain is not for the likes of you."

Victoria moved from behind Rose's chair to the side of the battered roll-top desk where she could face the woman. "Why?" she persisted.

Rose banged the pen on the desk, her attention finally distracted from the ledgers. "He is a wild one. It is said that he scalps and tracks like the Indians and rides like a Mexican. Latest rumors are that he has killed an unarmed man over some politician's daughter. Up in Austin."

"But this Steve Kaptain, he is a Texas Ranger, is he not? Why don't his commanders execute him—put him before a firing squad or hang him?"

Rose's round face broke into a knowing smile. "You sound bloodthirsty, *chiquita*. *Sí*, Steve is a Ranger, but General Scott can do nothing. It's said the general has raged and fumed like a volcano these past months, but Steve, he is not a regular. He's an Indian scout hired by Colonel John Hays himself. Whenever Steve feels like it, he disappears for a few months, and no one can do a damned thing about it."

"Where does he go?"

The fat shoulders shrugged. *"Quién sabe?* He probably returns to that rancho of his, hidden somewhere in the Sierra Diablo Valley. But some people say . . . bah! Only talk."

"They say what, Rose?"

"That the *hombre* is in cahoots with the Comancheros. But the Rangers need him too badly to question it."

The woman pulled out a cigar from one of the desk drawers and lit it. The first time Victoria had seen her smoking one of the cigars, she had burst out laughing. But Rose had asked, "Why can't a woman smoke, too, *chiquita*? We're human also, aren't we? Although, *Dios mio*, most men I've met don't seem to think so."

The smoke drifted about Victoria as Rose exhaled

and said, "Steve, he is a man that goes his own way. He's capable of anything, though, by the *Virgen Maria*, he does know how to treat his women." The sparkle in Rose's eyes was replaced by the usual businesslike shrewdness. "Nevertheless, *chiquita*, you steer clear of him, *entiendes?*"

And yet Victoria couldn't avoid him. There was the revenge she sought. Steve Kaptain was a Texas Ranger. And, she reminded herself, he had insulted her by implying she was one of Rose's girls. There would be some way she would yet even the score.

Some days later Steve requested tequila sent up to his room, and Victoria volunteered to Nita to take it. The thin, toothless old woman looked at her lasciviously and cackled. "So, Rose has finally let you learn the tricks of the trade, eh?"

Victoria shrugged, knowing Rose would fly into one of her lengthy tirades if she heard of it.

Her knees were weak when she knocked lightly on the door, and that peculiarly low, husky voice said, "Come in."

Whatever designs she had to wreak her vengeance, Victoria didn't know, but her plans were rendered useless by the other person in the room—a spare, sinewy man with sad eyes. He was dressed in fringed buckskins, and long brown hair grizzled with gray hung below a worn felt hat crowned with an eagle's feather.

The frontiersman and Steve sat hunched over the rickety table before the room's single window. Steve's back was to it, and sunlight streamed through the chintz curtains so that she couldn't see his face.

Particles of dust flurried in the slanting rays of the

afternoon sun as she crossed the room and placed the bottle of tequila between the two men. The two glasses clinked noisily when she set them on the table.

"Well, I'll be damned, Jake. It's the giant killer, my *courtesana pequeña*."

From beneath the heavily fringed eyelashes Victoria shot the younger man a murderous look. He laughed softly, and emerald glints of fire flecked his eyes. He said to his companion, "Rose has informed me Victoria here is off limits. Is that so, *bebé*?"

Victoria's startling light blue eyes met Steve's green ones. "For a crude *gringo* like you, *señor*, there is not enough money in all of Texas!"

The other, Jake, kept silent and leaned back in his chair, watching, but Steve laughed, and Victoria hated him more than ever for his arrogance. At that moment she earnestly wished she could take her knife and add one more nick to the myriad scars that marked the clean-shaven skin.

"Careful, honey, or I might be tempted to make you change your mind."

Before Victoria could spit back her contempt, he jerked one of the black braids again and said, "Now get along. We've got business to finish off—along with the tequila."

Jake's chair thudded to the floor as he reached for the bottle, and Victoria left the room with just as much rage steaming inside as before.

She was to see Steve Kaptain twice more that spring. It was a cool, star-studded Saturday night when she much preferred to be walking barefoot along the Rio Grande's pebbled banks. But the boardinghouse was packed, and Rose had enlisted her to serve in the back room.

The gambling room was thick with smoke and loud with raucous laughter. She set the tray of whiskey-filled glasses on the sideboard and turned to leave, when her eye caught the flash of a red bandana. More and more of the Rangers appeared on the streets those days, and each time she saw the familiar handkerchief, her breath locked in her throat.

Above the knotted red bandana, the tanned face studied the hand of cards before him impassively before flinging out a handful of coins. "I call you, Sam."

Behind Steve, Maya, a beautiful creole from Natchez with a satiny pink rose pinned to her coiled auburn hair, ran her fingers through the mahogany curls that lay at the nape of Steve's neck and bent to whisper something in his ear.

He gave her a one-sided grin as Sam, an aging cowpoke who showed up at Rose's every Saturday night as punctual as clockwork, threw in his hand on the green-baized gambling table. "Lady Luck rides with you tonight, Steve."

Steve looked up and began to rake in his winnings when he saw Victoria at the door. A slow smile creased his face. "She certainly does, Sam. She certainly does."

Victoria whirled and slammed the door behind her, hating the man whose gaze so mocked her and wondering why this particular Ranger stirred her to such fury.

Rose came upon her. "What is it, *chiquita*? You're breathing like a bull. Did some cowhand make a pass at you?" she asked, suspicious anger stirring in her voice.

"No," Victoria said, the lie resting on her tongue uneasily. "It's just all the smoke in there. It was stifling."

Rose nudged her chin affectionately with one brown fist. "See, I told you. This life isn't for you. Well, no matter. You won't have to go back in there after tonight. I'm getting me another girl. Some German hunker who's run away from home—some settlement up at Fredricksburg."

Rose was right. Victoria was never to return to the back room again.

II

✠✠✠✠✠✠✠✠✠✠✠✠

The next afternoon Rose was dead. Victoria found her slumped over her desk while the rain, driven inland by a Gulf hurricane, drummed a dirge on the dust-spattered window.

A wisp of grey hair had fallen across the smooth-skinned face. Victoria pushed the strand back and closed the boardinghouse ledger, putting it away in the bottom drawer.

She would not let herself feel the ache that lodged just below her heart like an arrow. Not until later. There was much to be done and no one at the boardinghouse capable of doing it. To Victoria, Rose's girls were empty-headed, frivolous creatures with no further thought than what color nail lacquer to use.

Locking the door behind her, she went to the kitchen and cornered Nita before setting off for the doctor. *"La patrona* doesn't want to be disturbed," she told the old woman, her golden-toned voice assuming a newly found authority.

"Got her an *hombre*, eh?" The rheumy old eyes glistened salaciously.

Barely able to check her disgust, Victoria consoled herself with the fact that, like the rest of the boarding-house's permanent occupants, Nita would find herself on the streets. True, Rose had talked often of her plans for Victoria when the girl was older, but now those plans were nothing but dreams to Victoria. Time had caught up with Rose.

Dr. Ricktor, who looked as skeletal as one of his cadavers, thought otherwise. "T'was the smokin', young'n. And the excess weight," he said, straightening and cramming the stethoscope in his black bag.

"What about the burial?"

"I'll take care of the details, young'n. You just get her dressed and ready."

Victoria was unsure about the proprietress's financial condition, although she assumed she was comfortably secure. "And the fee?"

Dr. Ricktor turned to her at the door. Admiration shone in his eyes. "You got a head on those pretty shoulders, don't you? I'll speak to old McBain. The only lawyer in town certainly ought to know how Rose's account stands."

The word of Rose's death seemed to have spread. When Victoria followed Dr. Ricktor from Rose's office, the girls had clustered outside the doorway along with some of the boarders. Victoria looked to the doctor, waiting for him to make the announcement, but he tipped his hat to her and continued down the hallway to the front door.

Turning back, Victoria encountered the group, their eyes fastened on her expectantly. Nita, the old witch—she'd surely claw her way to the top; Maya, her slanted golden eyes—like a cat, she'd always fall right side up; and the others—there wasn't any farther down they could fall, Victoria thought. Somehow they would all survive.

Victoria's gaze lighted on the runaway German girl, Eva. Although the girl was seventeen, the same age as Victoria, and much taller and better developed, she seemed younger. Those round blue eyes in the pretty baby-pink face were defenseless, the soft, trembling lips vulnerable. How long it had been since another helpless orphan had looked out at the world with such innocent eyes.

Victoria drew herself up and addressed them all, her full lips stretched firm in a stern mask. "Make your plans to leave. The boardinghouse will stay open tonight. Tomorrow it closes, and everyone will be expected to be out."

There was a sudden hum of voices like bees, but Victoria turned swiftly and escaped back into the office. She had no doubt but that the boardinghouse would be sold and the profits forwarded to Rose's sister and brother-in-law, the old man who had saved her at the river banks.

She leaned against the closed door and drew a deep breath. Before her Rose's body still slumped awkwardly, one hand dangling over the desk's edge. Straightening her shoulders, she crossed the room and began to make the necessary preparations. Rose, she knew, would want to be buried in her finest black silk dress, the one she reserved for Sunday mass and fiesta days.

The dining room was unnaturally quiet that night. Only a few customers dropped in for Nita's specialty, *lomo ahumado* and *puré de manzana*—smoked pork and apple sauce.

The girls had no clients and no prospects for later that night, facing the fact that not many would want to engage in sex in a house of death. They sat around the parlor, their usually vacant, painted faces wearing nervous looks.

It was near midnight when Nita and Victoria finished the dishes. The old woman for once was taciturn, and Victoria felt a pang of pity for her as she trudged off to her room. Even Miguel, the boardinghouse guard, lugging his rifle over his shoulder, had turned in for the night.

The bell at the front door rang softly as someone entered. Drying her hands on her skirts, Victoria went to see who could possibly want lodging that late at night.

A tall, lean man, broad of shoulder with narrow hips, leaned against the doorway, the moonlight framing him. Over one shoulder was slung a saddle.

"I'm sorry," Victoria said, "but we're closing for the night."

"I just got in, *corazon*. I heard about Rose."

Immediately she recognized the husky voice. It belonged to the Ranger, Steve Kaptain. "Then you certainly won't be wanting a room." Haughtily she turned to leave.

The saddle thudded to the floor as one hand shot out and grabbed her arm. "You aren't afraid of me, are you?" he asked softly, his voice holding a puzzled note.

In the hallway's shadows his face was all sharp angles and planes, and beneath the lowered brim of his hat his eyes had narrowed into green slits that studied her with a keenness she found disconcerting.

She pulled her arm away. "I'm afraid of no man. If you still want a room, I'll get the keys."

"Nope. Just stopped in to pay my respects to Rose. On my way north."

Effortlessly he heaved the heavy saddle over his shoulder, and Victoria realized she had been holding her breath as it released in an almost audible sigh of relief. Her hand was already on the door when he paused and said, "You got plans?"

The day had been so filled with things to be done that Victoria had quite forgotten where she would go after that night, what she would do. She stared back at the man, not really seeing him at that moment, as she tried to think of the future. What would she do? The realization that there was no one she could turn to, nowhere she could go, was overwhelming.

Dear God, but she was tired! The comfort of the broad chest and muscular arms was only inches away, enticing her beyond the tight control she had for so long imposed on her emotions. An unfamiliar sensation of languor swept over her.

Without being conscious of it she swayed toward him, and one arm swiftly enfolded her. As he swung her up against him, she heard, as if from a distance, the saddle fall once more to the floor. The faded blue

31

cotton shirt was soft against her cheek, and her weary eyes closed in delicious abandon. How wonderful to surrender, she thought; to feel the responsibility fall away.

"Which room is yours, Victoria?" he asked huskily.

"Upstairs in the back, the first one." Behind the darkness of her lids, everything seemed unreal. The same huskiness in her own voice, the booted foot shutting the door, the spurs that clinked softly on the steps.

She was aware again of his smell, the mixture of leather, tobacco, and the stimulating odor that was all masculine and undefinable.

Her door gave open, and she was next being lowered to the narrow cot that, together with the washstand and clothes hutch, were the sole items in the drab grey room—a large contrast to the velvety, plush opulence of the parlor below.

Slowly she opened her eyes. He stood over her, tall and scowling. The Texas Ranger she had tried to kill, the symbol of the sex she hated.

Even the tiredness etched in his face did not conceal the fires of passion that flamed to life in green depths of his eyes.

"Go away," she whispered.

The tiny lines on each side of the intently searching eyes deepened in a harsh grimace, and the long lids narrowed so that the smoldering eyes were almost invisible. "Don't play teaser with me, Vicky." The voice was soft, devoid of passion, but all the more frightening in its calm.

"I'm not what you think!" She tried to push up with her elbows.

With deliberate slowness he unbuckled his belt. "Oh? Let me be the judge, why don't you."

She attempted to struggle to her feet, but he shoved her backwards, and she fell helplessly on the hard, thin mattress. "Damn it," he said, the harshness grating in his voice, "what did you expect after the way you nuzzled me downstairs?"

She said nothing, but fought him with all her strength as his body lowered over hers. With her hatred overpowering even her fear, her long nails raked his back in twin red tracks, and her small, white teeth bit into his shoulder.

"Bitch!" he whispered at her ear before his mouth brutally sank into the satin skin of her neck.

Her slim body arched upwards in surprised pain. He took her without any further preliminaries, pinning her wrists to the bed and spreading her thighs with the overpowering strength of his muscle-corded legs. He took his time, slowing entering and withdrawing from her, all the while whispering Spanish sex words. Even as her struggling ebbed, the cadence of his breathing increased, so that his thrusts went deeper and she trembled with the unknown sensation that spread through her belly like warm honey.

As his release came, she heard him moan. *"Dios mio*, it's like drowning in you, *corazón*."

She looked up into the face furrowed with scars and saw the look of puzzled surprise. She spit at him then.

His hands tightened about her arms in burning brands, and the green fires of his eyes flamed to life again. "I don't know why you wanted to kill me that night, *corazón*, but the day'll come when you and I will have our reckoning."

33

"Bastardo!" she hissed. "Get out. Get out!"

He rolled easily from her and began dressing. "Whoever Rose was keeping you for, you sure weren't worth it. I've had better lays from a Kiowa squaw."

Her cheeks burned with shame as she struggled to pull her skirts down about her exposed thighs. "Good! Then I won't have to worry about being raped again by a stinking savage."

Steve chuckled. "A little she-wolf, aren't you?" But there was a touch of pity in his voice. He paused at the door. "Get your things together, Vicky. I'll take you as far as Corpus Christi. There should be decent work there."

Victoria sprang to her feet. "You've helped me enough! I can get along quite all right without you, Steve Kaptain!"

He shrugged. "Have it your way, *corazón.*" He touched the brim of his hat in mock politeness.

She could still hear his spurs clinking softly on the steps as the door closed behind him.

Sometime during the night Victoria was awakened by the muffled sound of sobs coming through the paper-thin walls. When the crying did not cease, she gave up trying to sleep. Slipping from her bed, still fully clothed, she made her way to the room next door, agonizingly aware of the pain in her bruised thighs.

"Ja?" a soprano-pitched voice asked in response to Victoria's knock.

"Eva? It's me. Victoria. May I come in?"

There was another muffled noise that Victoria took for assent. In the darkness, she closed the door behind her and crossed to the washstand, where she found the lamp and lit it with fumbling fingers.

As the light spread in growing circles through the small cubicle, Victoria made out Eva's voluptuous form huddled at the far corner of the cot, her face to the wall. Victoria touched her arm lightly. "Eva? Can I help you?"

The German girl shifted so that she was facing the petite girl she thought so beautiful, with her regal slimness and the thick, midnight-black hair that seemed to possess a life of its own. Realizing how awful she must look, her round Dresden-blue eyes swollen and red-rimmed, she hid her face in her hands. "I can't go back," she wailed. "I can't go back."

"It's going to be all right," Victoria said, sitting down beside her. "Don't worry, *niña*."

"*Nein*, you don't understand. I can't go back home. He'll sell me."

"Who'll sell you?"

Eva hiccoughed. "*Mein Vater*."

"Your father? But that's ridiculous!"

"*Nein*. I heard him tell Momma. She was crying and begging but he said it was the only way. There are eleven of us. And—our crop failed on account of the spring floods. He told Momma he had to sell one of us. And I'm the oldest!" Eva sniffed. "So you see, I can't go back!"

Victoria bit her lower lip, knowing she was being foolish if she let herself get involved. Especially when her own future was just as bleak.

"Don't worry about it tonight, Eva," she said and pulled the covers up about the other's trembling shoulders. "I've got a gold piece tucked away. We can make it somewhere on that."

But the bright sunlight of the next day didn't make the prospects for the two girls any brighter. And when it came time that afternoon for Rose's interment, the sky was overcast, as if foreboding events to come.

Victoria stole a look upward at the weeping Eva, who stood a good eight inches over her own five-foot frame. She half-regretted her impulsive gesture of kindness to the German girl, for she knew there was little she could do. And yet the gratefulness in Eva's eyes and the way she trailed Victoria, like a colt its mother, eased the responsibility that now hung about the smaller girl's shoulders as heavy as a prisoner's shackles.

Gritty dust, blown by a midday wind, stung Victoria's eyes, and she lowered her lids so that the newly formed mound and the feet of the half-dozen people who had showed for Rose's funeral were all that was visible.

She shed no tears, knowing that mysterious place tears come from had been walled off like Jesús Christos' tomb since that night long ago in Vallejo.

And, had she been able to cry, she doubted if she would have. Rose had been good to her, yes. But Victoria was shrewd enough to realize that Rose had a purpose behind her generosity. Only she had died too soon to see her purpose fulfilled.

The padre's voice droned on in Latin, and Victoria slid her hand into her reticule, feeling the security of the gold piece Steve Kaptain had tossed her. And yet she was frightened. She could see herself like Rose.

Old, alone, and desperate enough to try to live her life
again through a child. Victoria shivered as tumbleweed
suddenly rolled over the grave, reinforcing the loneliness that loomed before her.

III

✠✠✠✠✠✠✠✠✠✠✠

"Take it girl," the attorney urged.

Victoria looked at Leon McBain, a portly old man with graying hair and beard that spurted in all directions, debating with herself whether to accept the bills that lay in the outstretched hand.

"There's no strings attached. Rose had been keeping this account especially for you. It's not much, ninety-seven dollars. But it's something to start on. And her personal effects are yours to keep or sell as you wish."

Carefully Victoria reached for the extended bills. The money was crisp and wonderfully cool in her hand. She folded it and tucked it away in her reticule with the gold piece. The attorney's note, arriving immediately after the funeral, had been totally unexpected but certainly not unwelcome.

"Mr. McBain, I'd appreciate any advice you can give me. You see, I don't want this money squandered. I intend to become somebody with it."

McBain plopped down in the chair behind his massive pine-carved desk and rubbed his chin thoughtfully. "Well, girl, you are somebody—as far as I can make out. Don't know any other Victoria Romero. Nor anyone else that looks and acts like you do."

"I know I'm someone, Mr. McBain," she said, curbing her impatience, "but no one else does. One day I mean to make the name Victoria Romero dance on the tip of every tongue in Texas."

McBain's eyes squinted at her from behind spectacles that were as thick as bottoms of beer bottles. "That kinda depends on how you go about it, then, don't it? Whether your name dances—or dies in whispered gossip."

Victoria sat up straight in the hard-backed chair. "Exactly, Mr. McBain. Respectability is my goal. That and acceptance in Texas society. After all, I am half American. And I won't settle for less."

"Very commendable, girl. But as a man of many years, may I offer some sage words? There are some things that we can't change. The sooner we recognize this hypothesis—and accept it, the easier life is for us."

"You're not prejudiced, are you, Mr. McBain?"

"No. But I like to think I'm realistic."

"Well, so am I. And I don't give up easily. Will you help me?"

"I'm trying to, girl. But I can see you're hell-bent on

doing things your way. Same way, myself, at your age." He shuffled through some papers on his desk. "Ah, here the name is. Enrique Silva. A cousin of Rose's. He's an affluent banker in San Antonio. Rose left instructions for you to contact him, should you need further help."

McBain peered up at the young girl from beneath the rimless spectacles. "My advice, girl, is to hie yourself to San Antonio. Take enough money out of that bundle to live on," he jabbed a finger in the direction of her reticule, "and stash the rest away in Enrique's bank. Ask him to invest it for you. Then find work for yourself—respectable, of course. When you got enough pay stashed away, get yourself enrolled in the women's finishing academy there. Don't know what the hell the name is, but its name carries a pack of prestige. After that—you're on your own. And I've no doubt but that you'll succeed." McBain put out his hand. "Just don't forget the old geezer who pointed you on your way, girl."

But it was to be another several days before Eva and Victoria could find passage to San Antonio. The stage-coach made only irregular runs out of Reynosa north to San Antonio, but Leon McBain promised Victoria he would try to get the two girls a ride with anyone headed in that direction.

Victoria and Eva were forced to bide their time— each of them in separate ways. For free room and board, until a buyer could be found for the pillared monstrosity, Victoria kept the boardinghouse clean and ready for inspection.

Eva tried to help, but she was more of a hindrance, dropping dishes, scorching the curtains and sheets, crying at every turn. Her one fear was that her father would trace her to Reynosa. In the evening hours, beneath the dim light of the lamps, she would sit in the rocker, biting her already stubby nails.

Victoria also was impatient to be gone, but tried to find something to occupy the few free hours, for she could not allow fear or doubt to creep into her mind. She discovered some of Rose's black dresses that needed mending and set about making them over for herself. She silently promised herself that she would never again wear the *huaraches* and peasant skirt and blouse of the Mexican peon.

With one of Rose's made-over dresses and the new shiny black, high-buttoned shoes, Victoria had permitted herself to purchase, she looked several years older—and, she hoped, more dignified. She had taken to catching her heavy black hair in a bun at the nape of her neck. And if it weren't for the flashing blue eyes, which she reminded herself she would have to keep demurely lowered, she could pass for a very respectable schoolteacher. As yet, she was totally unaware of her vibrant beauty.

The first time Eva saw Victoria dressed in Rose's finery with her hair swept back, her soft pink mouth formed a large O from which no sound issued.

"Well?" Victoria asked, swirling in a circle so that the crinoline skirts swished loudly in the silent room. "Do you think I'll make a good impression on my next employer?"

"You're breath-catching, Victoria!"

"I don't want to be that," she said, and pulled on the snug white gloves. "I want to make the impression of an honorable, conscientious employee."

"Then you better wear a veil. Once some business-man catches sight of that creamy skin and—oh—pouting lips is the best I can describe them—he'll forget all about hiring you. One look in those blue eyes, and he'll have only one thing in mind," Eva tittered, "and that's getting—"

"Eva!" Victoria said, more sharply than she intended. "Remember we're ladies now!"

Eva began to cry, and Victoria crossed the room to quiet her with an impatient apology. It seemed to her that where Eva sought refuge in tears, she herself resorted to belligerence. Of the two of them, Victoria was practical enough to admit that she was the weaker, for she could not afford to lower her defenses with tears as Eva did. Victoria had to be strong when the cold ripples of self-doubt lapped at her feet like high tide.

Conversely, the natural spirit and zest that Victoria possessed were stronger than ever. But in those days of waiting, in preparation for the future, she forced herself into meekness, pressed herself into the mold set out for the laboring class.

His name was Benjamin Schneiweiss; a round, cocky Jew, small in stature and with thinning brown hair that straggled across his shiny dome. The stub of one arm, which he claimed he lost in a skirmish at San Jacinto, he waved in the air to punctuate his dialogue.

Along with a bitter-eyed divorcée returning to Connecticut and another German, a geologist, Ferdinand von Roemer, Ben shared the coach with Victoria and Eva.

He had eyes only for the sunflowered-hair amazon,

43

but Eva, under the onslaught of his obvious courting, was even more self-conscious than usual and bit nervously at her nails while her eyes darted about the rolling hill panorama that presented itself from the stage's windows.

The girls had spent three jouncing days traversing the one hundred miles that separated Reynosa from Falfurrias, the first way station at which stagecoaches made regular stops. The first night spent in the wagon bed had not been so bad, but the second night the girls and the driver, a taciturn middle-aged man who often drove to Falfurrias on his gunsmith business, were attacked by a swarming horde of voracious mosquitoes. The three finally gave up slapping at the persistent insects and continued in the darkened dawn on their journey.

At Falfurrias the geologist, the divorcée, and the one-armed Jew joined Victoria and Eva at the City Café to await the arrival of the stage. And it was there Ben began his dogged one-sided conversation.

When Eva sat mutely and the geologist and the divorcée refused to respond, he turned in desperation to Victoria. "Ever been to San Antone, miss?"

Slowly Victoria tore her gaze from the lush green countryside, so different from the barrenness of Vallejo and Reynosa, and gave the little man her attention. His aggressiveness did not bother her so much, for she unconsciously recognized in him a characteristic they both shared. She didn't know what to call it, but she did know that where some natures were crushed by overwhelming difficulties, others, like herself and Ben, were stimulated by them. And for this she admired him.

"No, never." Victoria shifted uncomfortably on the hard, wooden seat, eager for the evening when they would reach the Oaks way station and a comfortable bed.

"Same for me. But hope to start a restaurant there. I make the best sausage and kraut west of the Nueces, if I do say so myself."

Victoria noticed that Eva's attention was suddenly caught by the mention of familiar food.

"Yes sir," Ben continued, "I learned the secrets of cooking from my mother. Was a watchmaker. But when I lost my arm here"—he banged the stump on the coach's paneling—"I lost my trade. Took to cooking. I figure San Antone's the place to put in a restaurant. These days the town's bound to grow, it being the starting place and all."

"Starting place for what?" Victoria asked, her curiosity also caught.

"Why, haven't you heard? Gold's been discovered, miss. Yes sir. Saw the headlines myself in the New Orleans *Picayune* some months ago. Now men on their way to the gold fields stop off at San Antone. Last outpost of civilization. Town's bound to grow, like I said."

"You know how to make sausage?" Eva asked softly, her blue, limpid eyes round with pleasure. "German sausage?"

"Sure do, miss. My mother's from the old country, she is. Taught me to make the best damned sausage you'll ever taste.

Eva's closed face seemed to unfold like a spring flower in the sunshine of Ben's exuberance. The two lapsed into a mixture of German and English that Victoria was unable to follow. She noted though that von

45

Roemer's protruding eyes crinkled in amusement when Ben lapsed into his broken German.

The middle-aged woman never allowed the tight expression to slip from her face, but sat staring stonily out of the small window, and Victoria wondered why anyone ever bothered to marry if marriage brought so much unhappiness. But then, she reminded herself, her parents had seemed to be happy.

In the dying afternoon sun, where the pure and cold river snaked around a bend banked by three massive live oaks, the simple two-room cabin built of caliche blocks taken from the surrounding caliche hills stood like a fairy-tale palace to the five passengers who alit from the dust coated stage coach.

Victoria hesitated inside the doorway of the large main room, which was used for feeding the hungry coach passengers. She had seen the horses with the U.S. Army saddle bags tethered to the hitching post outside and was expecting an assembly of noisy soldiers within. But there was a sudden hush as she entered. Nervously she gripped the handle of her carpetbag and looked around for someone in charge. Experience had taught her that soldiers in a group were to be avoided.

"Howdy, ma'am. Can I be of service to a purty woman like yourself?"

Victoria turned, startled. In the dimness of the cabin her eyes focused, and she saw the gritty soldier with the thatch of corn-colored hair protruding from beneath the stained cavalry cap. He turned and winked at four more soldiers grouped around one of the long wooden tables placed against the wall.

One of the soldiers took a long swill from the uptilt-

46

ed bottle he held in his hand and, wiping his mouth on his sleeve said, "Hey, Walker. Let me service her!"

There was a guffaw from the other men, and Victoria took a tentative step backwards, only to bump into Eva and the other passengers, who had just crowded inside the door. She drew a deep breath and said, "Where's the couple who run this station?"

The soldier called Walker swaggered over to her. "Why, I told you, ma'am, I'd be glad to help you."

"Ist Herr Dunlop hier?" Von Roemer asked, trying to force some bluster into his reedy voice.

Walker looked over at the geologist contemptuously. "You know, boys, I do believe we've got ourselves a turtle-eyed foreigner among us."

There was more laughter from the soldiers. Victoria felt herself pushed aside as Ben stepped forward. His face purple with anger, he shook his stump at the grimy soldier. "Here, you! Show some respect for *die Damen* present!"

"Hey Walker," a gangling-looking soldier called as he rose from the table unsteadily, "did you hear something?"

"Yeah!" Walker snarled. "Another foreign pipsqueak!" He grabbed Ben's stump and twisted it cruelly. Ben gasped.

The other soldiers began cheering, and Eva shrieked. The coach driver, a small, wiry man called Adams, tried to pull the women back from the scuffling.

"Aren't you going to help him?" Victoria demanded of the driver.

"What can I do, lady? There's too many of 'em!"

Victoria shrugged off his restraining hand. Without

thinking what her actions could cost her, she swung her carpetbag toward the soldier's thick body. Instantly she regretted her impulsiveness. The soldiers had been merely taunting the civilians, but now, because of her foolishness, she saw their attention turn to her, their eyes crawling over her like fat hairy caterpillars. She shivered.

The Walker man grinned slowly, a lewd smile displaying yellow chipped teeth. Abruptly he released Ben and grabbed at Victoria. His odor assailed her nostrils. He obviously had not bathed nor shaved in weeks.

"Got a lot of spirit, eh, filly? Well, I'll be more than glad to break you in."

Victoria went rigid as one hand fastened brutally on her breast. Slobbery lips ground against her mouth. Released from her paralysis by her indignation, she pounded clenched fists against him.

Her struggling infuriated him, and he drew back a hairy fist. Eva broke from the group and tried to assist Victoria, but the man sent the German girl sprawling instead with a resounding cuff.

"Sergeant Walker!"

IV

✠✠✠✠✠✠✠✠✠✠✠

Everyone's eyes were riveted on the doorway. Framed against the sunlight was a soldier of medium height with broad shoulders. He passed through the group clustered there and made his way toward Victoria and Walker, who still held her in his grip.

In one part of her mind Victoria noted the cleanliness of the man's uniform as contrasted to the other soldiers, and the hard, level gray eyes that looked so out of place against the amiable countenance, which was sprinkled lightly with freckles.

"Sergeant Walker," he said, "we don't need any

trouble here. Do we?" His voice held a subtle implication of something else.

The other eyed him sullenly but released Victoria. "Yes, sir," he grunted.

"All of you," he said, addressing the other soldiers. "Water and tend your mounts."

Sheepishly the soldiers shuffled outside as the group of civilians parted for them, and the man turned towards Victoria.

"Lieutenant Ted Garrett, ma'am," he said, removing his hat. "I offer you my most sincere apology for this—unpleasantness."

Numbed, Victoria could only nod her head while Ben bent to help Eva to her feet.

"Where are the Dunlops?" Mrs. Neil asked, pushing forward. "The couple that are supposed to run this station."

"We was beginning to think maybe your men up and murdered them," Adams said.

The lieutenant's face was grim. "I wouldn't put it past these men, but the Dunlops are safe. I just returned from taking Mrs. Dunlop to her sister's home down the road. Her sister's—" He paused with a disconcerted expression. "She's expecting a baby shortly. Unfortunately," the officer hurried on, "Mr. Dunlop, I understand, is away on business. I'm sure they're sorry about this inconvenience to you all."

Victoria thought the gray eyes beneath the golden hair kind and said softly, "We owe you our thanks, Lieutenant Garrett."

"My pleasure, ma'am," he replied, turning his full attention to her again.

She looked directly up into the fine-featured face

and saw with surprise the admiration openly displayed there. Up until that moment she had not realized that she was attractive. Neither was she aware that she possessed a vibrant type of beauty that would attract men all her life, being both a blessing and a curse to her.

She forced herself to turn away from the disarming smile as Ben said, "If *die Damen* will help me, I'll prepare our meal."

Knowing full well that Ted Garrett's eyes followed her, Victoria rolled up her sleeves and began helping. Eva set two tables for everyone while Ben fried beef and beans. Victoria offered to bake biscuits, and, to her surprise, Mrs. Neil joined them.

Hair flying, the woman whipped a batter for pound cake, using the last of the eggs Mrs. Dunlop had collected that morning. She seemed more congenial as she related to Eva and Victoria the story of her earlier life in the Far North, where snow fell in six-foot drifts and lakes froze over so one could skate on them.

By the time dinner was served, the soldiers returned, and the relaxed atmosphere became tense once more. There was little talk, mostly of the weather—how the hot summer seemed to have suddenly set in although it was only May. The only other sounds were the grunts of the men eating and the scrape of knives on tin plates.

Dinner over, the men rose and ambled outside. Eva, Mrs. Neil, and Victoria were left alone to clean up the mess and prepare the room for the night. Blankets were thrown over the long tables. The men would sleep in the large room on these tables, and the three women would have to share the Dunlops' bed in the smaller room. Realizing there wasn't enough room for the three of them in one bed, Victoria volunteered to sleep in the loft, where a few thin, narrow mattresses were kept for extra boarders.

The men came shuffling back inside, and Victoria noticed how Ted Garrett's eyes searched her out. It was her first experience with romance, and she sighed gently as she put away the last of the pots. She would have liked to linger, but, like Eva and Mrs. Neil, she felt slightly nervous in the presence of the soldiers who had bullied them. Although Ted had the senior rank, Victoria instinctively felt that it was a thin control he kept over the hotheaded group. As the driver, Adams, had pointed out, one man could only do so much.

Reluctantly, Victoria retreated with the other two women to the cabin's smaller room. Bidding them good night, she took the lantern and climbed up into the loft. Clad only in her shift, she blew out the lantern and stretched out on one of the mattresses. For a while her thoughts drifted, always returning to Ted Garrett. The warm eyes set against the gold tones of his hair and face, the polite manners, the way his gaze rested on her.

She was almost asleep when she became aware of her skin itching. It took several minutes before she realized the mattress was infested with bedbugs. Finally giving up, she rose and quietly slipped down the ladder. From the larger room she could hear the occasional snort and snores of the men.

Silently she crossed to the door and lifted the bar. The warm night air rustled through the black hair tumbled about her shoulders, and she breathed deeply, feeling instantly renewed. She was alive and healthy and—even pretty, she thought, or Ted Garrett wouldn't look at her like he did. She stretched, savoring the feeling of contentment. In the moonlight her body was outlined through the thin shift, revealing its slim suppleness, the perfectly rounded breasts, and the long, well-shaped legs.

Victoria heard the sharp intake of breath and whirled. A form stepped forward. "Sorry, ma'am. Didn't mean to frighten you," Ted said softly. "I couldn't sleep either."

Aware of her state of near undress, Victoria wrapped her arms about herself. "I—I didn't know anyone was out here." She moved to go back inside, and he put out a hand as if to stop her.

"Please don't go, ma'am. I'd enjoy talking with you. My men and I have been out in West Texas for some months now, and it's been a long time since I've had the chance to talk with a woman, excepting a few of the soldiers' wives, that is." Victoria knew it wasn't proper for her to remain, but she was moved by the earnestness in his plea. After a moment of indecision, she nodded her head in assent.

"Would you care to walk down to the river? After the deserts around Fort Davis, I can't seem to get enough of looking at water."

Victoria smiled shyly. "I know how you feel. I grew up in a small town that was also surrounded by desert. There's something peaceful about flowing water."

Together, but not touching, they moved down toward the sloping banks of the Leona. The faint trail moved through prickly scrub trees and brush that occasionally encroached on the path. All round them crickets chirped, and from the river ahead of them came the throaty croak of a bullfrog.

Through a part in the brush, Victoria saw the Leona, glimmering with the diamonds of the moon's light, and she caught her breath. It was a moment of magic, of moonlight madness. She felt Ted take her hand.

"Tell me something about a soldier's life," she said, afraid to continue that wondrous moment.

After a moment he replied. "It's a lonely life. The pay's poor, and the food's bad."

Victoria laughed. "Then why did you join?"

He led her toward a rocky protuberance where they seated themselves, still slightly apart, overlooking the river. There was the sound of its gentle lapping against the mossy banks and the fresh scent of juniper and willow trees.

"I come from a wealthy Virginia family which thought it highly improper if you didn't become either a doctor or a politician. A disgrace to the family's good name. But that kind of life bored me. Instead of going off to college as an obedient son should, I rebelled. I broke and ran. And the military took me in."

"Do you regret your decision?"

"Only the financial aspect," he said, his face suddenly grim in the moonlight. "But somehow, one day, that'll take care of itself," he added, his voice now light.

"After having had so much, is military life terribly uncomfortable?"

He laughed. "There are only two things considered uncomfortable by mounted men of pluck. To be in the rear of a charge—or behind in a retreat."

Victoria smiled, and he noticed for the first time the

small dimple in her rounded chin. As if entranced, he stretched out a finger and touched it. "There is one thing other I regret," he said quietly. "That my time's not my own. That when I find someone as lovely as you—"

He broke off and bent over her small upturned face. Victoria did not move as his lips gently caressed her own. His arms slid over her shoulders and pulled her to him. For a long moment their lips clung, then his own released hers and began roaming over her face. Kissing her closed lids, the curve of her high cheekbones, and moving on to the small recess of her delicately shaped ear.

Victoria gasped as she felt the tip of his tongue touch the hollow of her ear. The tightening in her stomach was a new, frightening feeling. And yet, she couldn't pull away as his lips continued their journey down her throat and came to rest on the soft mounds of her breast that were visible just about her shift.

She heard his own heavy, ragged breathing and abruptly came to her senses. "No!" she whispered, drawing away and scrambling to her feet.

Instantly contriteness crossed his face. "I'm sorry," he said, reaching for her. "I forgot myself."

But Victoria turned and ran, her betraying heart pounding loudly in her ears. Within the safety of the loft, she sagged weakly onto the mattress. Why, she wondered, had she never realized the power of passion? To think that she could lose her will, her self-control, so easily. And what must Ted have thought of her? She was half afraid to face him the next morning. Yet eager.

In the early light of dawn, Victoria rose and dressed.

With a light heart she went below. When Adams, who was already up, informed her that Lieutenant Garrett and his men had ridden out long before, Victoria's small oval face closed over, never once betraying her thoughts.

Whitewashed stuccos and wooden lean-tos appeared on the horizon, their miniature forms dwarfed by the few rising brick buildings that indicated San Antonio's growing prosperity.

By the time the stagecoach rumbled into Military Plaza, Ben Schneiweiss had both courted and proposed to demure Eva, and had been accepted. That the two would live together until they could afford to marry did not greatly shock Victoria; for Eva had nowhere else to go but back to the brothel. But also there was the fact that Victoria herself had to admit—that she had come a long way from the cherished and protected young girl who had spent a brief part of her life in the old-world manner of her parents' *hacienda*. That old-world existence, which had held such charm, was nothing more than an illusion to Victoria.

Mrs. Neil, who had thawed during the long journey, and Ferdinand von Roemer were continuing their trip onward to Austin together. Victoria said her farewells and smiled somewhat sadly as Eva and Ben told the divorcée and her companion, the geologist, good-bye. It seemed to Victoria that chance could be a good matchmaker ... but only for some people.

Carefully lifting her skirts out of the rising dust, she descended in front of the renowned Menger Hotel and looked about the plaza. Directly across from the hotel was the San Antonio First City Bank, of which Enrique Silva's father had been the founder and late president. Victoria was tempted to call on Rose's cousin immediately, but it was after five and she was sure he probably would not be in.

Resolutely she turned back to the hotel and picked up her carpetbag, her back straightening in determination.

"Victoria?"

Victoria looked up at the large-boned girl, whose eyes were misty.

"I'll miss you, Victoria," she said tremulously.

The smaller girl set her carpetbag down, chastising herself for her unthoughtfulness. "Oh, Eva. I wish you and Ben the very best."

She gave the big girl a hug and stepped back, choked at the parting. "Take good care of your Ben, or I'll see to it that every Mexican *bandido* in the vicinity raids your new restaurant."

Ben laughed and wrapped his good arm fondly about Eva. "My *Schätzlein* will protect me!"

Momentarily Victoria wished desperately that there was someone to protect her, for it had been a long time since she had felt so lonely, standing in front of the cold, impersonal hotel.

The room was just as impersonal, perhaps because it had been the cheapest the ogling desk clerk had to offer. Victoria stood before the mirror over the notched and burned old chest of drawers and brushed out the waist-length hair, the repetition of the strokes easing her worries.

Dear God, what if she did not find employment? It was a foolish risk she had taken. But surely, because of her years in the convent, she had more education than most young ladies forced to earn their own wages. Surely she could act convincingly enough the part of a schoolmistress or tutor.

She realized she would have to fabricate some sort of reference, but she would worry about that when the moment came.

A sense of adventure welled in her, dispelling her disappointment over Ted Garrett. She told herself that what had happened would serve as a good reminder of the male's perfidy and hoped that the same did not happen to Eva, though Ben seemed sincere enough.

She slept deeply for the first time since Rose's death, with a stubborn confidence in her abilities to drive away the fretting worries.

V

✝✝✝✝✝✝✝✝✝✝✝✝

The hot, coffee-colored eyes beneath haughtily arched brows glanced down at the writing before him and back again to Victoria.

"A previous employer, you say, señorita, recommended my name to you?" He flicked the paper with his slender, brown fingers. "This woman, Señora Pelton. Her name is unfamiliar to me."

The voice of the suavely dressed man across from her had a silky smoothness that did nothing to conceal the suspicion which hovered in its tone.

"By way of Leon McBain, her attorney, Señor Silva." Victoria let a touch of impatience lightly color her own voice. "As I explained, Señora Pelton knew she was about to die. Though she wasn't wealthy, she left me a small amount of money, with the instructions that I should seek out her attorney should I need help. It was Mr. McBain who recommended San Antonio and your bank. He felt I could make a new start here; that your bank would use good judgment in investing some of my inheritance, as you may call it."

Victoria had no intention of letting Enrique Silva know she had once worked for his cousin. That part of her life she was determined to put behind her. Just as her existence in the convent was nothing more than a dream now. The fabricated Señora Pelton would serve her purpose—a reference for Victoria. And should the banker check out her story, Victoria knew Leon McBain would back it up.

Enrique Silva's eyes passed over her, as if weighing the situation. She sat primly in the brocaded, stuffed chair, hoping to appear older and dignified. "I also would like to find some manner of work . . . to occupy my time, of course."

"Of course." He raised one brow, and a slight smile played about his lips. "I would like to help you, but I have no idea what kind of work would be suitable for what you seek. You see, Señorita Romero, there is a big demand for hired help here in San Antonio, but it's for maids, waitresses, and such. I doubt if this is what you have in mind, *de veras*?"

Victoria compressed her lips to still their trembling. If she didn't find a job soon, she could well be destitute by the time she paid her hotel bill. She needed work immediately. "I'm seeking any employment, Señor

Silva, that will allow me to live independently—and respectably."

Enrique studied her over long, brown finger tips that met together in an arch. "You realize, Señorita Romero, that even here in San Antonio people of Spanish descent sometimes have difficulty in finding social acceptance."

"You have apparently broken the barrier, señor."

He smiled thinly. "So I have. But then I was fortunate enough to be born the scion of a prominent family whose name has been highly respected by the citizens of San Antonio for more than a century."

"Yes," she replied grudgingly, "that does make a difference."

Enrique rose and crossed to the window. From his second-story office he looked down on the cobbled street that bustled with businessmen. His aristocratic hands were clasped behind his back, almost hidden by the fine lace cuffs.

There was something about the girl, he thought, that made her different. He had known other women just as beautiful, but their insipidness had revolted him. There was a warmness, a vitality about the girl that intrigued him. Perhaps this time it would be different.

Slowly he turned and faced her. "You have no other relatives to turn to?"

She shook her head mutely.

"Permit me to help you then. I plan to marry early next year and will need help with the supervision of the festivities in the meantime—someone to oversee the preparations. A sort of glorified housekeeper. Would you be willing to take on this responsibility? The position in my household would be quite proper for you."

Did she imagine the irony that tinged his voice, she wondered. She hesitated. The offer was a windfall, yet . . .

"Don't let the thought of impropriety worry you, Señorita Romero. My cook, Consuela, who's deaf but quite reliable, and Pedro, the houseboy, also occupy my home."

A small sigh of relief escaped Victoria's parted lips. "I feel the arrangement would be most satisfactory. When shall I begin, Señor Silva?"

The middle-aged man with the distinguished gray that mingled with the dark-brown hair at his temples went to her and took one small, gloved hand. "Enrique, please. I don't wish any formality in my household. Only a comfortable friendship between us all."

"Enrique, then."

He pressed a perfunctory kiss on her fingertips. "I'll have a carriage sent for you tomorrow." He bowed low. "Until then, Victoria."

In spite of Enrique's apparent kindness, Victoria's innate mistrust of the male sex was strong enough to keep a guarded distance between herself and her new employer. She had learned enough of man's lust not to be careless. Yet Enrique's manner, except for one incident, was formally polite, if just as distant, those first weeks. And that one time, she was sure, had been unintentional.

"I hope you've found it pleasant working here, Victoria," he had said, coming upon her in his library. He had given her permission to catalogue his books when she had explained to him that her supervisory duties didn't keep her busy enough.

Surprised, Victoria turned on the small stepladder

on which she was precariously balanced. Enrique put his hands around her waist to steady her, and her own hands caught at his shoulder. For a moment neither moved.

Then Pedro the houseboy, a slim-flanked youth with a pockmarked face, appeared in the doorway of the library. "Señor Silva, your carriage has been brought around front."

"*Gracias*, Pedro," Enrique said shortly, releasing her.

Turning back to her, he said, "*Perdóneme*, Victoria, there is a dinner party I must attend." He was handsomely dressed in skin-tight breeches that flared about his dress boots, a short black velvet jacket, a *bolero*, over a white linen shirt, and a flat-crowned sombrero sat at a rakish angle on his head.

That was the only time that summer he stepped beyond the bounds of propriety. Yet she noticed he gradually seemed to spend more time in her company.

Those first months passed slowly, with few visitors calling at the Silva house. Rather the homes of other wealthy families opened their doors to Enrique, where he was feted almost nightly in what Victoria knew would be lavish style. For there on the frontier that isolated San Antonio there was little to entertain the denizens other than those dinner parties.

During this time she took the opportunity to learn the decorum of San Antonio's society—who the important people were, where to seat the ones that would be regular guests, the courses more generally preferred at the dinners, and the numerous other details that made entertaining successful.

It was with a certain pride that she continued to run

the house, more efficiently, Enrique declared, than any of his other housekeepers. Consuela, a thin, timid-looking woman in her seventies, seemed relieved to have someone take over those duties of a housekeeper, which she had been trying to keep up with.

"*Sí, sí!*" she would shout, as if Victoria were the one who couldn't hear and not herself. "Colonel Hays *quiere su carne así,*" and point a bony finger at the blood-rare steak she was preparing on the *parilla.*

From the brick oven came the sweet smell of *pan dulce,* making it hard for Victoria to concentrate on the myriad questions she needed answered. It was those times in the kitchen that she thought of Eva and wondered how she was faring at the restaurant. She had noticed with a certain homesickness the small announcement in the San Antonio *Light,* which Enrique brought home each evening, that the German girl and Ben had applied for their marriage license.

If Consuela was relieved, Pedro was resentful that Victoria should assume some of his previous duties. Victoria saw to it that fresh linens were laid out daily for the master's bed, that candles were replaced as soon as they burned low, that scented soap and clean towels were ready, and that the lamps were kept filled with kerosene. While Enrique was most particular about his personal grooming, he took little interest in the cleanliness of the house. Victoria gave the rooms their first thorough cleaning in many a month.

Pedro allowed her those menial duties, but was most adamant that she not touch his master's gun case in her tour of dusting. She was aware that Enrique took a special pride in his firearms and that the youth shared his pride. Pedro would lovingly caress the dull metal and dark wood as he shined the guns and rifles to a luster finish.

Enrique seemed mildly pleased with the improvement of his household and even took time to instruct Victoria in answering the many invitations that arrived at the house. By the end of August she was addressing invitations herself—for a tea Enrique was holding the following Sunday afternoon in honor of his fiancée, Alice Farrington. Her parents and a few close friends the engaged couple shared were to be invited.

Victoria was seated in the dining room the latter part of that week making out the market list when Enrique entered. "I've been looking for you, Victoria. I'm spending the day with a friend, and I wanted to make sure I'd given you enough money for your marketing before I leave. Will you need to make any extra purchases for Sunday's affair?"

Victoria was pleased that he trusted her with the household finances and was determined to keep her expenditures at a minimum, though there certainly wasn't a financial need to do so.

She shook her head. "No, Enrique. I believe everything's under control. I just hope that the tea is successful. I want your betrothed to be pleased."

Enrique's lips pressed together in a thin line. "Having a female in the house as beautiful as yourself, Victoria, may raise some problems."

"What is she like, your fiancée?" Victoria knew she shouldn't ask such a personal question, but she couldn't restrain her curiosity. Enrique never mentioned her and seemed to have only the slightest interest in his courtship of her. Then there was also the fact that Victoria would be working for this woman, at least until she had saved enough from her wages to attend the finishing school.

"Alice Farrington," Enrique answered, "is a very elegant young lady. The toast of San Antonio. Her family's name, I imagine, is as old as mine." He permitted himself a slight smile. "And I know for certain, as wealthy."

Victoria wondered why Enrique had waited so late in life to marry but attributed it to his pecular fastidiousness. "I wouldn't be concerned about my presence upsetting your fiancée, Enrique. I plan to make myself most inconspicuous."

His dark eyes assessed her briefly, but Victoria remained composed, not at all flustered, for Enrique's somber irises lacked the lust she had read in the eyes of other men. "You have a maturity about you, Victoria. Yet Alice can't be much older than yourself."

Victoria's smile was brittle. "I've had a different life than your fiancée. I'm inclined to suspect that experiences rather than time dictate one's age."

"You remind me much of my *compadre*, Antonio Morales—who should be here shortly. His sharp wit amuses me greatly—as yours does."

Victoria couldn't repress a shiver. The man called at the Silva home often, and she found there was something about him that was repulsive, though she couldn't put her finger on it.

The great brass knocker clanged heavily against the double front doors, and Pedro suddenly appeared, gliding through the *paseo* to admit the caller.

At the sound of a soft, tenor voice, Enrique bowed low in Victoria's direction, always the *caballero*. "If you'll pardon me, I must go. *Hasta luego*."

66

Not wishing to have to speak with Antonio Morales, Victoria rose also, murmuring she had some duties to attend to upstairs.

The wrought-iron railing was cool beneath her hand as she ascended to the second floor. The squarish, sun-whitened stucco home overlooked the San Pedro River and was one of the few two-story structures she had noticed in San Antonio's elite district. Enrique, she felt, was justifiably proud of it. One day, she promised herself, she would possess such a house.

Nearing the top, she glanced backward in spite of herself. The two men were in the *paseo*, preparing to leave. The older man, Morales, held her attention. His movements, as he adjusted the flat crowned hat over the thick ivory hair and wrapped the long cape once more about the mounds of fat that enveloped him, were incredibly graceful for such a massive man.

He whispered something, and Enrique laughed softly, throwing a companionable arm about the other's shoulders. "Antonio, your suggestions are most lascivious!"

Inexplicably, Victoria felt guilty, an intruder listening in on a conversation not meant for other ears.

In the midst of the shared joke, Pedro inadvertently dropped Morales' malacca cane. Victoria saw the pale blue eyes in the fleshy pink face shoot the houseboy a blistering look of contempt. *"Pendejo!"* Morales hissed.

Victoria's black taffeta skirts rustled as she turned from the embarrassing scene below, but not before she witnessed the three pair of enigmatic eyes jerk upward to follow her departure.

She tried to shake the incident from her mind. But later, as she rode with Consuela to the market square in one of the two open buggies Enrique kept in the carriage house, her blue eyes came to rest on Pedro, who was driving, and the small nagging began again. Though dressed in the loose, white cotton garments of the houseboy, Pedro's behavior certainly did not seem out of the ordinary.

The colorful sights of the city finally drove the scene between Morales and Pedro from her mind. The buggy found its way along the narrow, winding cobblestone streets of San Antonio's old district, then passed through La Villita, the shantytown of the poorer-class Mexican families. Here Victoria turned her eyes away, not wishing to be reminded that she possibly would share the same sort of future should she not achieve her goal.

Consuela pointed out with a gnarled finger the Spanish Governor's Palace, an impressive building surrounded by luxuriant foliage, and the ruins of the mission now called the Alamo after the Spanish word for the cottonwood tree.

The buggy rattled over a wooden bridge which showed signs of neglect. Below, young Mexican girls were bathing nude in the San Antonio River, and in spite of herself Victoria blushed, though Consuela and Pedro seemed unaffected by the sight.

Most of San Antonio lay on the right side of the San Antonio river banks, and it was there in the main square that the buggy finally rolled to a halt. In the marketplace stalls were jammed together. Vendors hawked their wares; old women and ragged street urchins sat before brightly colored blankets laid out on the ground and piled high with fresh fruits and vegetables. The acrid smell of plucked chickens, skinned pigs, and stale fish permeated the air.

It was a place of excitement, color, and noise. Victoria never failed to enjoy herself on market day. It was with reluctance that she concluded the last of her purchases and began the trip back. They had recrossed the wooden bridge into the old part of San Antonio when the buggy was forced to pause along the side of the street to allow a troop of mounted men to pass. Always uncomfortable around soldiers, Victoria watched with disdain as the two lead soldiers rode past and tipped their hats courteously in her direction.

With them was another dressed in fringed buckskins, and her breath drew in sharply as he looked her way. His gaze fixed hard, but she met steadfastly that insolent stare of amusement underlined with sexual interest. Steve's sun-darkened fingers lightly touched the brim of his hat as he passed her by, his fathomless sage-green eyes flashing with mockery.

She was shaken more than she cared to admit. She found the man detestable, hating him with a loathing that made her tremble for the way he had used her.

VI

❀❀❀❀❀❀❀❀❀❀❀

The last of the guests had left, and though it was still early in the evening, Enrique had retired to his study with a decanter of cognac, his face etched with tautness.

Victoria knew that, on the surface, the tea had seemed to be a reasonable success. Hors d'oeuvres were served with hot Manzanilla tea, and decorated petits fours graced the ivory laced table, which she and Pedro had moved into the center of the *sala* or living room. Everything had seemed to run smoothly.

Except for one ill-timed moment. Pedro had been busy, and Victoria answered the door to admit more arriving guests. An elegantly dressed young woman and an elderly couple faced her in the doorway, and she instantly knew the young woman to be Alice Farrington, accompanied by her parents.

In spite of her polite manner, Alice made no attempt to hide the withering look in her narrow-lidded hazel eyes. "You must be Enrique's little housekeeper, Vic—"

"Miss Romero," Victoria replied evenly, and stepped aside to admit the three people.

While she waited, Alice took her time removing her beribboned cloak and the carnation-pink chip bonnet that sat on her head at a saucy angle, revealing honey-colored curls clustered on top her head. Negligently she passed the cloak and bonnet to Victoria.

Her eyes were the color of frosted cucumbers as she said sweetly, "Enrique is most appreciative of your services, and I know I can depend on you to serve me as efficiently, can I not?"

Victoria remained silent, afraid her voice would reflect the unaccountable dislike she instantly felt for the young woman.

Alice's father, a stout man with a walruslike mustache, said gruffly, "Come along, Alice. Your friends have been kept waiting long enough." He grabbed her elbow and that of his overdressed, bewildered wife and pushed them forward.

Enrique, stylishly handsome in a black cutaway, hurried toward Alice and her parents with outstretched hands and a warm, welcoming smile. Alice lifted a pale cheek to receive his light kiss, and her parents smiled fondly, anticipating the social and financial rewards Enrique Silva would bring to the Farrington household.

Victoria had turned away, thinking the afternoon was going to be all right after all. But later Consuela gossiped that she had overheard Alice and Enrique arguing in the library. So Victoria was not surprised when Enrique morosely shut himself away in the library after everyone had departed.

But she was shocked when late that evening, after she had finished putting away the fine china and had extinguished the lights, she passed the library, with the candlelight peeping beneath the door and Enrique suddenly jerked it open.

"I was wanting to see you," he said thickly.

Expecting him to give notice of her dismissal because of something the disgruntled Alice may have said earlier, Victoria drew back her small shoulders. "All right," she replied and stepped around him, entering the library.

As she turned to face him, her hands calmly clasped before her, she noticed the near-empty decanter on his desk. "What is it you want of me, Señor Silva?" Purposely she emphasized his surname, reestablishing the employee-employer relationship.

Without warning he grabbed her to him. "I want you," he cried.

Victoria tried to push him from her, but he held her tightly to him. "Oh, Victoria, *cara mia*. Victoria! Don't you see? You're my only hope!"

She looked up onto the olive face, now mottled by the evening's heavy drinking. A look of bewilderment shone in her eyes, and he shoved her from him. "*Carramba!* You don't understand, do you?" His voice was, all at once, weary. "Go away, Victoria."

He returned to his desk and slumped in his chair.

Brandishing one ringed hand in the air, he said, "Go to bed. I'm sor—sorry about this. Better tomorrow morning."

Slowly Victoria backed to the door and let herself out of the room.

And the next morning Enrique *was* better, never mentioning what had happened the night before. Victoria took his cue and went about her duties as if nothing had happened either, though she feared another such outburst. She realized she would have to make her plans soon. But it was Indian summer in San Antonio, and the weather was much too beautiful to be preoccupied with Enrique's unexpected display of passion.

However, one golden afternoon shortly thereafter Victoria finished her work early and took the opportunity to slip away, although she had Enrique's permission to take off whenever she wished. She deposited the seventy-three dollars she had saved from her wages in her reticule and frowned as her eyes alighted on the gold coin at the bottom of her hand bag. Reminders of Steve Kaptain invariably tied her stomach in knots.

Pushing the thought of him from her mind, she crisply told Pedro to drive her past Military Square to the Spanish Governor's Palace; that she wished to see some of the sights of the city on her own. Actually she hoped to gain an interview with Madam Rochester at St. Ursuline's Academy. If she was accepted, the seventy-three dollars would be a deposit for the following semester's tuition.

When the buggy arrived before the great stone building aged by time, she instructed Pedro to return for her in two hours. He nodded respectfully, but Victoria stepped back involuntarily as the houseboy raised eyes bright with malice. Hurriedly she turned away and, pulling her black shawl tighter about her shoulders, set off in the direction of the academy, three blocks from the Governor's Palace, Consuela had told her.

She had gone but a few steps when she suddenly recognized with delight the female figure moving toward her. "Eva," she called.

"Victoria! I've thought about you and tried to find out where you went. Ben and me searched through the newspaper and asked everyone that came into the restaurant about you. What happened to you?"

The narrow street was thronged with people, and Victoria drew Eva into the sheltering doorway of a pawn shop. "There's not much to tell, Eva. I'm a housekeeper for Enrique Silva, the president of First City Bank here. But I want to hear about you—and Ben. Are you married yet?"

Eva put up her hand and flashed the simple gold ring at Victoria. "Ben and me married two weeks ago. We live in back of our restaurant—on Travis Street." The Dresden-blue eyes looked at Victoria beseechingly. "Tell me you'll come to visit us. You was my best friend, Victoria."

Victoria took Eva's large, work-reddened hands between her two small ones. "I promise you, Eva, I shall try. Now I have an appointment I must keep. Will you give Ben my regards?"

Eva declared she would, and the two reluctantly parted. Victoria turned once, watching the tall girl disappear down the street, and was momentarily envious of Eva's good fortune. Eva had someone to care about.

She wasn't lonely. And someone obviously cared for her.

But Victoria refused to be depressed. All that she had been working toward was only a few blocks away. Acceptance by St. Ursuline Academy would mean she was halfway along the road to becoming the lady of quality her mother had been, the lady of quality she had vowed to old McBain she would one day be.

After the golden afternoon sun, the parlor of St. Ursuline's Academy was chill. A thin, reedy woman with small, close-set spectacles on her pinched nose ushered Victoria inside, and Victoria explained to her that she wished to talk with Madam Rochester, the directress, about attending the academy. For twenty minutes Victoria sat in the horsehide chair the woman had shown her to and stared out the one window, curtained with dull green tasseled draperies. The parlor was well furnished, with a drop-leaf mahogany writing table, green and gold Sheraton chairs, and a Victorian walnut sofa, but Victoria found the room lackluster and the hushed atmosphere tedious and was relieved when the woman finally returned and led her down the central hall to the directress's office.

Mrs. Rochester, wearing a brown serge dress of good cut, rose from her desk. Because of her proper English background, the woman was retained as directress by the academy's board. With good reason the board realized that San Antonio's upper-class families, made up mostly of influential Mexican families like Enrique's, would want their daughters to attend an academy headed by such a person as this slim, middle-aged Englishwoman. Anything that smacked of England assured San Antonio's citizens of quality.

Above the polite smile the Englishwoman's sharp eyes looked over Victoria. "Miss Romero, won't you be seated, please."

Victoria took a seat in one of the chairs the woman indicated. After the directress had resumed her seat, Victoria said, "Mrs. Rochester, I am interested in attending your academy."

The Englishwoman folded her hands on her desk. "Saint Ursuline's is pleased that you've considered our finishing school, but I must tell you that there is a waiting list. And the tuition is somewhat steep."

Victoria's heart sank. It wasn't only her desperate drive to rise in the rank of society that now stood in jeopardy, but the unavoidable fact that she would soon be without a job or a place to stay, once Alice married Enrique. The young woman's intense jealousy had been all too evident the afternoon of the tea. She most certainly would make life unbearable for Victoria.

"Just what is the tuition, Mrs. Rochester?"

The Englishwoman was impressed by Victoria's determination, expressed in the square chin and the steady gaze of the sea-blue eyes. But it was the girl's demeanor; her dignity, the self-respect that suggested the girl came from a family of quality, the old world charm that barely covered the volatile woman beneath, which brought the Englishwoman to decide in the young woman's favor.

"Our tuition is two hundred and fifty dollars a year, Miss Romero. But the academy will accept installments with the provision that the entire tuition is paid by the time the student begins."

Victoria left the red stone building with a receipt for her seventy-three dollars in her reticule. True, she was on a waiting list for entrance for the spring semester, but with only ninety-seven dollars remaining in Enrique's bank she would need that time to save the money from her wages in order to have the needed two-hundred-and-fifty-dollar tuition.

Fall passed, and with the advent of the winter season, usually mild there in San Antonio, Enrique began to entertain more often in his own home. Although Victoria became adept at overseeing these functions, she never failed to be chilled by Alice's icily polite presence.

Victoria watched the guests closely, marking their social manners, not that mannerisms were much different than the etiquette she had been instructed in as a child. Reared by her father, a proud *hacendado*, and her mother, with her gentle English manners, Victoria discovered she had more elegance and class than most of the young ladies who were raised on that primitive Texas frontier.

And, watching them, she vowed again that the day would come when she would take her place among them, indistinguishable from those elite except by her tough inner core that had produced a liveliness that was markedly absent in many of the vacuous faces present. Victoria wondered if wealth, high birth, and good looks produced weaklings instead of the gods she had imagined those people to be.

There was at least one among Enrique's friends that was far from her idea of a weakling, though there was certainly nothing about him that she could find to admire. Rather, it was a sinister power that exuded from Antonio Morales that in some way frightened her.

One night in particular she recalled, when Enrique

had entertained late. Antonio had remained, and the two of them had withdrawn to the library. Enrique requested that Victoria bring them a bottle of wine and two glasses.

When she entered with the tray, Enrique said, "I was just telling Antonio, Victoria, how I was so fortunate to acquire your services."

"Yes, indeed," Antonio said from his overstuffed high-backed chair. "Though it is quite distressing to learn that you are all alone in the world . . . with no friends—no relatives."

Victoria found herself unable to meet the large man's piercing blue eyes, and dropped her gaze to the ruby-red liquid in the wine glasses she carried. She started to utter something about her friends Ben and Eva, but for some reason caution sealed her mouth. "Will there be anything else?" she asked, and set the tray on the desk.

Enrique shook his head no, and Victoria retreated from the room, uneasily aware that two pair of eyes watched her leave.

Enrique did not entertain again until the first week in December, when he held his Grand Ball. Victoria discovered that even those of the upper class suffered spasms of nerve attacks. Two hours before the guests were due, Enrique fired a volley of questions about duties which he ordinarily entrusted to Victoria without qualm.

"Did you hire the *mariaches*, Victoria? You know— the ones that play at Military Square on Saturday nights?"

"Yes."

He paced the *sala* from one end to the other. "And

79

did you order enough wine—the *alcalde*'s favorite—oh, what . . ."

"Chateau du Plesis? Yes, we have enough for ten balls."

"Muy bien. Muy bien." He paced the room again. "And the carnations for the ladies?"

"There's one long-stemmed carnation wrapped in each dinner napkin, Enrique."

"Muy bien," he muttered, once more preoccupied.

With a little over a half hour remaining before the party would begin, Victoria escaped to her room. She looked with revulsion at the four or five black dresses in the clothes hutch. Never had she been so sick of black. For that reason alone, she said to herself, she would never consider being a nun—like Mother Teresa, who had always seemed like a giant crow swooping down on Pedro and herself.

There was nothing she could do to change the color of her dress that evening, but she wrapped a fine beige lace shawl of Rose's about her shoulders and caught her hair up atop her head, camouflaging the pins with one of the pink carnations she brought up with her from the kitchen. Pinching some color into her cheeks, she could see the hint of beauty reflected in the tarnished mirror she faced. The slightly tilted, startling blue eyes set in the cream complexion and framed by heavy straight hair as black as turbulent skies.

It was a contrast that was eye-catching. Yet she hoped, incorrectly, that no one would notice an insignificant housekeeper.

As large as Enrique's house was, it appeared that Pedro would be forced to close the door to any further guests, so packed and overflowing were the rooms by midevening. But the guests continued to arrive, spilling out into the gardens, which seemed to be the most popular place.

Here the *mariaches* serenaded the elegantly dressed couples standing about the flagstone patio or seated at the scattered tables which had been moved outside solely for that purpose. Surrounded by lush tropical plants and trees, there was an atmosphere of romance quite different from the gay laughter and bubbling conversation that came from within.

For a moment Victoria gazed wistfully at these couples, but returned her attention to her duties, moving on past the patio doors toward the kitchen. But Alice intercepted her and tersely informed her that she wished Victoria to be posted at the front door to help the arriving guests with their wraps, though few brought any, so mild was the December evening.

Sighing, Victoria let her intended duties go neglected and moved toward the *paseo*. Her progress through the *sala* was hampered by the crowd, so that she burst free from the stifling room with relief—only to freeze like a doe before the hunter.

VII

✤✤✤✤✤✤✤✤✤✤✤

His presence filled the *paseo*. The dark green eyes swept the room boldly, at once absorbing everything and revealing nothing. He was dressed stylishly in a smoke-gray suit and hand-cobbled boots from the best leather. A black Spanish-style hat sat low over the slightly curling mahogany hair.

It was a far cry from the rough garb of the frontiersman or the simple, coarse clothing of a Texas Ranger, but Victoria would have recognized that rugged countenance anywhere.

"Steve Kaptain!" she breathed audibly.

Several guests overheard her and turned to look as

83

the tall, lean man's intense gaze came to rest on her. The well-chiseled lips suddenly smiled in unconcealed amusement.

With him, dressed in a broadcloth suit, was a thin gentleman, equally as tall, with lively blue eyes and a Roman nose. Someone near Victoria whispered, "Isn't that Rip Ford?" The name jumped to other lips, and the man next to Steve made a sweeping bow.

"Yes, ladies and gentlemen," he said merrily, his voice loud even above the hum of conversation, "I'm *the* Rip Ford. Lawyer, doctor, soldier, politician, explorer, newspaperman—at your service."

The crowd applauded enthusiastically and opened to receive the two men after they had passed their hats to Pedro. Steve moved toward Victoria, and she raised her chin proudly. Her eyes narrowed with suspicion. "What are you doing here?"

"I might ask the same of you, *corazón*."

"Won't you introduce me to your lovely friend, Steve?" Rip Ford asked.

"Certainly. It's my pleasure to present to you Victoria Romero." He smiled lazily down at her, well aware of her fury she was attempting to keep under tight control. "You might say, Rip, that Miss Romero and I share the same fondness for weapons."

Before Victoria could make a biting reply, Enrique, with Alice clinging regally to his arm, came forward to greet the new arrivals. *"Mis Amigos*, welcome to *mi casa*. May I present my fiancée, Alice Farrington."

Alice smiled formally at the two tall men, but her hazel eyes, to Victoria's surprise, came to rest on Steve with a distinctly calculated interest.

"Mr. Ford here," Enrique continued, "and Mr. Kaptain, along with Major Neighbors, are planning an expedition west to El Paso. And I'm hoping, dear, to bribe them into accepting me as one of their investors for their venture."

Alice looked at Steve pointedly and said, "I'd like to try my powers of persuasion over dinner. Mr. Kaptain, would you be willing to escort me into the dining room?"

Steve's long lips parted in a knowing smile and the penetrating eyes responded openly to her invitation. "With pleasure, Miss Farrington."

Unaccountably, Victoria was furious that Steve ignored her.

"Miss Romero, are you with anyone?" Rip asked.

Victoria brought her attention back to the two men at her side. "Why, no, but I'm—I—"

"Excellent!" Rip presented his arm. "Will you do me the honor of being my dinner partner? I won't take no for an answer."

Victoria looked to Enrique in confusion, but he merely nodded his assent distractedly as his narrowed eyes followed his fiancée and Steve Kaptain.

Hesitating, Victoria slipped her arm in the crook of Rip's elbow, allowing him to lead her to the dining room with the other guests. Three long tables had been moved into the dining room, and to Victoria's chagrin she found herself and Rip seated across from Alice and Steve. Victoria was not surprised that Alice never took notice of her inclusion in the party, so engrossed was the woman with the sun-bronzed man next to her.

At the far end of the same table Enrique took a seat a few moments later, a plump matronly woman on one side and a horse-faced debutante on the other. At another table Victoria saw the immensely fat, ivory-haired Antonio Morales in deep conversation with a young man dressed ostentatiously in purple velvet. She immediately decided that, if forced to make a choice between two evils, she would readily have chosen to be seated across from Steve Kaptain rather than Antonio Morales.

Rip Ford's loquacious wit highly entertained her, and she gradually relaxed and enjoyed herself. His hands stroked and molded every phrase as he described to her his service with General Taylor in the Mexican-American War.

Since he didn't seem to take the war between the two countries personally, Victoria in turn did not feel compelled to defend the country of her birth, even laughing delightedly as Rip recounted one of his amusing adventures in Mexico.

She presented a cool, composed demeanor, in spite of her initial nervousness, bringing envious looks from the women and admiring ones from the men. Her soft, startling beauty was enhanced a hundredfold by the glint of intelligence and humor in her light blue eyes.

Once she caught Steve's eyes, in that seemingly perpetual half-closed look, watching her, and he smiled wickedly as her own eyes blazed her dislike at him.

Haughtily she turned back to Rip. "Tell me more about these Texas Rangers you served with."

The man was not fooled by her sudden interest. He had intercepted the looks that had passed between his friend and the incredibly lovely girl at his side. Rip was well aware that his friend possessed a raw virility which invariably attracted every female. He found it highly amusing that Steve seemed indifferent to the women who attempted to employ their female wiles in his presence.

Rip looked down at the petite young lady next to him. He sensed there was something stronger than friendship between Steve and Victoria in spite of her obvious irritation with the scout. It would be interesting, he thought, to watch the struggle between those two strong personalities, and knew that the outcome was one bet he wouldn't wager on.

Realizing Victoria was waiting for an answer, he said, "The man who hopes to become a Texas Ranger, my dear, must have a complete absence of fear. For him fear and courage are unknown. He is not conscious of either."

"What you are saying contradicts itself, Rip."

"No really. Since the Ranger is not conscious of either fear or courage—he is free to act in complete accordance with his intellect. He is free to combine boldness with judgment."

"And do you think that really applies to all Rangers?" she asked, the contempt flashing in her eyes.

Rip glanced at Steve, who seemed to be listening intently to what Enrique's fiancée was saying. "That is one question I don't believe I should risk answering, Victoria. You'll have to decide that for yourself."

"I already have," she said, her expression suddenly enigmatic. "Will you excuse me, please, Rip?"

With sad eyes Rip watched the young lady move among some of the other guests who had finished and were heading in the direction of the *mariache* music on the patio. It had been a long time since he had thought of his dead wife and experienced the pangs of loneliness this girl had aroused within him. He perceived the warmth and passion beneath the cool exterior and rightly supposed that life would never be boring with her for a companion.

Victoria went directly to the kitchen and checked with Consuela, who was still busy serving up the delicious cinnamon-flavored *flan* for dessert. "Señorita Victoria," the old woman shouted distractedly, "what will we do? There are too many people and not enough dessert!"

Victoria patted her stooped shoulders. "Don't worry," she shouted back, "many of the guests have already left the dining room for the patio. They seem to prefer music to dessert."

Victoria herself couldn't resist the lure of the Spanish music. It brought back memories of fiestas her father had staged in the large courtyard of their *hacienda*. A time, she reminded herself bitterly, that should be forgotten.

Noting that everything seemed to be running smoothly, she allowed herself a few minutes to edge along the lantern-lit garden wall where, from the darkness of one corner, she could watch the dancing guests. Something within her stirred—a longing for she knew not what—as she followed their movements to the slow, romantic chords of a flamenco guitar.

"And has Cinderella found her Prince Charming?" a deep, low voice whispered at her ear.

She whirled to find Steve at her side, one hand resting high above her head against the stucco wall. There was a negligence in his stance, yet she knew he was intensely aware of her. The probing eyes glinted like shards of green glass in the dim light.

"If I have, it certainly isn't you." She picked up her

skirts to move around him, as if stepping around filth in the streets, and Steve grabbed her arm.

"You're haughty as a *hidalgo, corazón*!"

She bristled. "And is there anything wrong with a little pride?"

"Only when you become so touchy you start looking for trouble when none's there."

She would have pulled away then, but his hand tightened, and he swept her up against him in a fierce embrace, moving her out into the midst of the other dancing couples.

She knew she was trapped. She couldn't make a scene there, but was forced to suffer his nearness. Though, after the first strained moments, she found dancing with Steve strangely pleasurable. He moved with a grace peculiar to frontiersmen, holding her against him so that she shared his movements and was one with him during the haunting melody.

Neither of them spoke, observing the truce that existed between them while the music lasted. She forgot her hatred of him and relaxed within the strength of his arms.

"You've changed, Vicky," he whispered into the feathery curls at her ear. "My little wild kitten has become a sleek feline."

"I'm not yours," she muttered emphatically.

"You're wrong there." The violins and guitars faded out, and he led her back to the dark, secluded corner when the musicians launched into another song. The musky scent of jasmine and hibiscus enveloped them as he bent low over her. "You *are* mine. I made you mine in Rose's boardinghouse."

"How dare—"

He broke off her furious protests as his lips lowered over hers, moving softly but firmly. Different from the brutal kisses he had forced on her before.

She made a halfhearted attempt to push him from her, but he drew her closer, holding her body tightly against the length of his, so that she could feel the hardness of his chest and the taut flatness of his stomach.

At last he released her, and she leaned against the wall, breathless, glad of the support of the cool stones.

"The question is," he continued, his voice light and sardonic, "who has made you since, Vicky?"

Victoria gasped at the pain inflicted by his insult. Her hand came upward in a luminous arc, slashing across the mocking face. "*Bastardo!* You are the only—"

Steve caught her up against him, his hand cupping her head against his chest and muffling her words. "I'm sorry, Vicky," he said gently. "That's none of my damned business."

She shoved him from her, tears she had not thought possible springing to her eyes. "*Hijo de puta!* You are like the rest of the *chacals*! Turning your own foul deed on the woman—as if I had been responsible for that night. You're no better than . . . than a dog in heat!"

She whirled from him, fleeing the soft, mocking laughter.

VIII

✠✠✠✠✠✠✠✠✠✠✠

It was a disastrous mistake.

Victoria had received word from Mrs. Rochester that there would be an opening for her at the academy on April 1. Jubilant, she planned to give Enrique her two-weeks' notice that evening after dinner. But it was nearing midnight before she had finished with her duties, and when she went to the library, discreetly knocking at the door, there was no response. Thinking that perhaps Enrique had fallen asleep, she gently opened the door.

Antonio Morales and Enrique were clasped in a passionate embrace, Antonio's mouth obscenely closed over Enrique's. At first Victoria didn't understand. Then, filled with disgust, she began to retch, her stomach heaving violently in dry spasms.

Antonio whipped about, surprisingly agile for so large a man. *"Puta! Que pasa—?"*

The baby-pink complexion grew purple with outrage. He advanced on her, his face contorted with a threatening malevolence. Victoria backed slowly toward the door. Antonio was faster. He shoved it closed with a tremendous thud. At the same time one heavy arm locked itself about her neck.

"Enrique!" she begged between gasps.

Enrique jerked his head toward her, her plea arousing him from his languorously drunken stupor. With swaying steps he came toward the two. Antonio's solid arm wrapped tighter about Victoria's throat. It seemed to her that the room was spinning crazily—as if it were being tossed about by a hurricane that darkened everything.

"Antonio! Wait!"

Victoria felt Antonio's hold loosen as Enrique pulled on his lover's arm, and she gasped with relief as air suddenly soared back into her lungs, searing her bruised throat.

"We can use her in a better way," Enrique suggested, his slim hand resting lovingly on Antonio's velvet clothed shoulder. "A threesome could be quite—quite entertaining."

Victoria felt herself reel then, as the two faces, greedy with lust, turned on her. Both caught her between them, leading her toward the sofa. She was like a corpse in their hands. But as Antonio shoved her face downward, she began to struggle wildly. Panic rose in her, suffocating her like swamp water. She heard the sleeve of Rose's black taffeta dress rip, and she found the breath to scream.

But her echoing screams were drowned out by the shattering blast of a gun.

"No!" Enrique's yell was full of anguish. "Antonio!"

Victoria tried to rise from the sofa just as Antonio's faceless body fell forward on her, the blood splattering over her like a cascade. Enrique grabbed at Antonio, tears streaming down his slim, distinguished face, and Victoria was able to extricate herself from the two intertwined men. It was then that she saw Pedro in the doorway. One of Enrique's rifles hung from his hand. An odd smile twisted his acne-blotched face.

"There won't be anyone else for you, Señor Enrique. No one to come between us." His voice was like the hissing of a serpent. Slowly he glided toward Enrique, who had ceased his sobbing and watched the youth with terrified fascination. With his free hand, Pedro began to stroke Enrique's wavy brown hair.

Realizing Pedro and Enrique were momentarily oblivious to her presence, Victoria slipped past them, rushing down the hallway and out into the chilly night air.

How long she ran, she did not know. She followed the San Pedro River into town. The twisted roots of cottonwoods and willows tripped her, and once she stepped into the frigid, muddy slosh of the river's bank. At last she could see the few house lights of San Antonio's late revelers shimmering between wind-tossed tree limbs. Most of the streets were dark as she scurried along like a frightened deer. Hugging the store fronts, her heels clipped against the boardwalk like ghostly echoes.

An old drunkard stumbled out between two buildings, and she screamed. "Ma'am—hey, ma'am." The raspy voice, rank with alcohol, drifted up from somewhere beneath the shabby hat. "Could you spare an old soldier a few coins?"

"No. No, I'm sorry," she said, backing away from the trembling hands that clutched at her torn sleeve. "I don't have any money with me." She held her breath, waiting.

"Oh," he mumbled dejectedly and turned away.

Like the blow on the head of an amnesiac, the encounter brought Victoria to her senses. She looked around her, recognizing the area. She was near the place where Eva and she had met, three months earlier. She could see the dim outline of the Spanish Governor's Palace rising above the other buildings a block away. Only a short distance farther was Travis Street. Somewhere along it was Eva's and Ben's restaurant. Victoria began running again, but this time with a purpose in mind. Her eyes darted from one side of the street to the other, trying to discern in the darkness the names of the building signboards.

From somewhere down the street came the faint clip-clop of horses, and Victoria went rigid, realizing it might well be Enrique and Pedro searching for her. When she saw the long line of pack mules straggling toward her, her fears faded. Still, she knew it was only a matter of time before the alarm would be raised. Antonio Morales's death could not go unnoticed for long.

At the same moment, her eye caught the name of a signboard directly opposite her. *Ragouts*. She remembered once Eva had raved about her mother's stew, calling it *ragout*. Victoria was forced to wait for the mule team to pass, before she could cross the street. More slowly, her heart beating anxiously, she approached the restaurant's door. It was dark inside.

She knocked lightly. When there was no response, she summoned her courage and pounded loudly. Soon lights shone from beneath the door at the rear of the store. When she saw Ben come out, dressed in a red flannel robe and nightcap, relief flooded through her, and she felt her body go limp as a wet noodle.

His one good arm held a lantern above his head as he peered out into the darkness. Setting the lantern on a nearby table, he went to the door and lifted the bar. Cautiously he cracked the door and looked out.

"Victoria!" he exclaimed, opening the door wide. "*Mein Gott!* What has happened to you?"

So happy was she to find Ben and Eva, she had completely forgotten her dishevelment. Quickly she pulled the loose sleeve up about her arm and tried to smooth the stray curls back into place. From the far door Eva appeared, sleepy but concerned. "*Wer ist es?*"

"Come in," Ben said, "come in." He turned back to Eva. "It's Victoria, *Schätzlein.*"

Eva hurried toward her then. "Victoria! Look at you!" Eva's hand came away with blood. "You're hurt!"

"No, it's not mine, Eva." Victoria felt suddenly weak and very tired. "I'll explain it all to you later. But do you have somewhere I could sleep for the night?"

"How did this happen?" Eva asked.

"Will you two women stop gibbering," Ben broke in.

95

"It's morning already. *Schätzlein*, get some blankets and a pillow for Victoria. I'll drag out the cot."

The short, rotund man hurried ahead of them as Eva led Victoria through the restaurant, which was soaked in the aromas of dumplings, sausage, wheat beer, and cabbage. Behind the dining room was a smaller room with one large bed. In one corner stood a bureau with a pitcher and basin on it. "Would you like to clean up," Eva asked, "while I get bedding for the cot?"

"No thank you, Eva," Victoria answered wearily. "I'm too tired."

There was only the one room behind the restaurant, but Ben set up the cot in an alcove formed by the hutch and bureau, his one arm functioning faster than some men with two.

"There you go, Victoria. Now lay yourself down and get some rest."

Victoria looked over at the rumpled bed. "Aren't you two going back to bed?"

"It's 'bout time for Ben and me to start aworking on the dumpling dough and the stews. We've done had enough rest. You're the one that needs it now." Eva pulled the covers up about Victoria's shoulders, and Victoria wondered sleepily how she had ever thought Eva a helpless child.

Bright sunlight was streaming through the one window, high on a cracked wall, when Victoria awoke. She lay there a few moments, trying to recall what had happened and where she was. With the recollection came the pain, as she cleared her throat. Not only was her throat sore, where Antonio had tried to strangle her, but her entire body ached as she moved to rise.

The mirror over the bureau presented a pale young woman with purple shadows beneath her eyes and hair tumbled about her shoulders. She was washing her face when Eva entered.

"I heard you stirring, Victoria. Are you hungry? Did you rest well?" Her eyes were evasive, and Victoria knew by the way she rushed her words, unusual for the placid German girl, that something was amiss.

"Is something wrong, Eva?"

"Oh, Victoria. It's awful. There's a warrant out for your arrest. They're hunting all over San Antonio for you."

"Arrest? For what?"

"For the murder of Antonio Morales." Eva looked down, unable to meet Victoria's eyes. Her hands plucked nervously at her apron.

Victoria turned back to the mirror and began pinning up her hair, trying to gain time to think.

"How can you be so calm? Oh, what happened, Victoria?"

"I'll tell you later, Eva. Right now, I need a message delivered. Can you do it for me?"

"*Ja.* Ben will take it, while I serve the customers."

"Good! I'll need some paper."

It was foolish, she knew. Even as she wrote the note in terse sentences she cursed herself. But there was no one else to turn to. She couldn't stay there at the restaurant. Sooner or later, she would be discovered. And with her, Ben and Eva could be implicated for the crime.

Victoria took up a pack of cards and began playing solitaire on the cot. But as the afternoon dragged by, she found it hard to concentrate and gave up. Instead her thoughts turned bitterly inward. How she had worked doggedly through the lonely Christmas and the cold winter under the speculative eye of Enrique and the harsh, icy glare of Alice—only to lose everything. Because of her stupidity, her plans had all gone awry.

She told herself she should have recognized the obvious. That Antonio Morales was a homosexual. Along with Pedro and Enrique, incredible as it seemed to her. There had been a pimp, she remembered, who hung around Rose's. Rose had warned her the pimp was different from other men. Although at the time Victoria didn't understand, she now could see the similarity in the pimp to Pedro.

She thought about her opportunity to attend the academy, now lost to her, an alleged murderess; about the money she had so painstakingly earned, all deposited in Enrique's bank or with the academy, and now inaccessible. Using every curse word she had heard at the boardinghouse, she flung the cards from the cot, scattering them across the floor.

Eva came in then, her wide blue eyes taking in the strewn cards. "Oh, Victoria," she said, closing the door against the chatter coming from the customers in the restaurant, "please don't worry. I just know everything'll be okay."

Embarrassed at her childish outburst, Victoria sprang from the cot and stooped to gather the cards. "I'm sure you're right, Eva," she said contritely. "But everything seems to look so hopeless right now!"

"Everything looked hopeless to me when I was at Rose's. But because you took me under your wing"—Eva smiled broadly—"like a little mother hen, why look what I have now."

She spread her hands to encompass the small room. "A husband, a place of my own, and a very good friend that I still haven't repaid for the coach fare to San Antonio."

Eva went over to the bureau and, pulling out a drawer, withdrew a small, rectangular wooden box. Opening the lid, she took out several bills of paper currency.

"No," Victoria said, crossing the room to Eva. "I don't want your money. You and Ben have paid me back a hundredfold by taking me in and hiding me. Keep the money for that baby you said you always wanted."

Eva bent over and gave Victoria a peck on her cheek. "You just wait, Victoria Romero. One day all the good things you deserve'll come your way. I gotta get back to the tables now."

It was almost evening before Ben located him. The door swung open and as quickly shut before Victoria could even turn around. The two of them were alone in the dim room. Steve crossed the room and lit the lantern.

"You took long enough," she said, trying to hide the relief in her voice.

One dark brow raised in sardonic amusement. "Out looking for you, *corazón*. Thought I had turned this town upside down, but I damned never thought of this restaurant."

"Then you heard?"

He swung the only chair in the room around backwards and straddled the seat, resting his arms on its back. "Yep. You sure look a hell of a mess." The tiny weather lines about his eyes crinkled in a smile.

"Is that all you can say?" She bounded from the bed in fury finally released. "When everyone around me is asking about what happened, and—and all you can say is some biting remark about how I look!"

"Does it matter what happened? I figured you were in trouble and would need help." He moved to rise. "But then guess I was wrong."

"Oh!" She stamped her foot in exasperation. "What do you want me to do, Steve Kaptain? Beg? Okay, then. Yes, I need your help."

Steve resumed his seat. But the half smile left his long mouth. "If you want my help, Vicky, you're going to have to do what I say."

She had forgotten how green those eyes were. In the light from the lantern they gleamed like molten emeralds. Her breath caught in her throat. "Just what does that mean?"

"Just what I said. Do I have your promise?"

She faced him, belligerently refusing to submit to his demand. "Well?" he asked. "What's it to be?"

Both of them knew she had no other choice. "You have my promise," she answered thinly.

"Sit down. I'll go over this only once. It's important you remember everything I tell you. Because I won't see you again until the time comes for us to leave."

She nodded. The relief of letting him take over swept over her, and she settled back on the cot.

"I take it your friends are completely trustworthy. I'll give them a list of supplies you'll need."

"For what?"

"You're taking a trip. A long one—to El Paso."

"El Paso?"

Steve nodded. "Yep. Since gold's been discovered,

the whole nation is clamoring for a passable road west. I've been commissioned to find one to El Paso. Robert Neighbors and Rip Ford are meeting me north of here in two days—at Brandt's trading post, with about fifteen other wagons and a couple dozen pack mules. It's going to be a hard journey. Think you're up to it?"

"Of course," she snapped. "But what's in El Paso? What am I to do when we get there?"

"Thought you to be a pretty independent female. You'll figure out something by the time you get there. The problem right now is getting you out of San Antonio. I'll be by for you the day after tomorrow. I want you dressed in boy's clothing. Understand?"

She wanted to refuse, but it was hardly the time, she thought, to get on her high horse about propriety. "I'll be ready."

"Good." He rose to go and came over to the cot. She looked up at him, wondering why he, of all men, should so disturb her.

"Is that all?" she asked, forcing a coolness to her voice she was far from feeling.

"No. I'll expect payment."

"I don't have a penny," she said flatly. "Should I sell myself to someone along the way? Maybe an Indian friend of yours would need a squaw for a day or two?"

Steve grinned. "I don't think that drastic a step will be necessary. I'll take my payment in some other way."

"Oh, you—"

"Hasta luego, corazón." He tipped his hat low over his eyes and strode from the room before she could think of anything hateful to say.

IX

✼✼✼✼✼✼✼✼✼✼✼

The stars crackled in the frosty sky above them, and Victoria pressed herself even closer against the broad expanse of Steve's back, seeking a shield against the night wind in the warmth it offered. The smooth jacket next to her face smelled of leather and sweat and age, but there was a comfort in the masculine odors.

"Cold?" he asked over his shoulder.

She shivered as the wind whipped about them again. "It's my bottom that hurts more."

"You'll get used to it. There's a lot more riding ahead of you."

They had left San Antonio after dark, when there

was less chance of Victoria being recognized or questions asked. It seemed to her as if they had been riding the entire night, though the pumpkin-colored moon was not yet high in the heavens. The great trees that rimmed San Antonio's outskirts had given way to rolling, treeless prairie, intensifying just how alone the two of them were.

As they continued to ride through the night and no words were spoken between them, Victoria began to wonder what the silent man in front of her was thinking. Was there a sweetheart, she wondered, or a wife somewhere waiting for him? But it hardly seemed likely. Steve Kaptain didn't appear to Victoria to be the type to be tied down to one woman.

And, as certain as she was that there were many women who shared his embraces, she didn't plan on being one of them. She readily believed that he would not hesitate in demanding his payment for rescuing her, and she intended to make sure it was not in the flesh. Somehow she planned to find another way to repay him.

And that brought her full circle again to her predicament. She was where she had started from, almost a year ago—penniless and without prospects of employment. Her mind began to weave dreams and schemes. She would not give up, she vowed. But soon lethargy overtook her, and the repetitious swaying on the horse gently lulled her to sleep.

A few moments later she lurched suddenly, grabbing tightly about Steve's lean, muscle-corded waist.

"Vicky?"

"I—I must have dozed off," she mumbled, wide awake now and disliking the idea that she had weakly succumbed to sleep while Steve, who rode his Appaloosa as if he were part of it, was still very much alert—and, she knew, very much aware of her arms wrapped tightly about him and her slim body pressed closely to his.

If he was aware that she just as suddenly released her hold of him, he gave no indication. "We're halting at the grove of trees just beyond the next hill. There's a small stream there. Can you make it?"

"Of course I can."

In less than fifteen minutes Steve swung off the great roan animal dotted with black leopard spots. He caught Victoria about her waist, lifting her down beside him. When he did not release her, she looked up to meet the green flecked eyes. For a long moment the moon burned there in their emerald depths, as hot and bright as the noonday sun.

Roughly she shoved away from him, breaking the tension of the moment. Steve chuckled lowly. "So you've returned to being the little wildcat." He picked up one of the sticks lying about and handed it to her. "Then you can start digging a trench for us."

"For what?"

"To sleep in."

"Hell'll burn itself out before I sleep with you!"

He gave her a crooked smile. "Have it your way," he said, and strode away from her, disappearing out of view in the darkness.

"Where are you going?" she called softly, but he didn't answer. Dumbly she looked down at the stick in her hand. She felt like throwing it at him, so sure was he of himself. It was irritating. Yet she had to accept this role of domestic servant he imposed on her. At least, she thought, until they were far enough from San Antonio.

Her hands were numb from the unusually cold March night, but she began digging in the soft earth. The hole was barely large enough for one person to sit in when Steve returned, his arms loaded with mesquite brush.

It seemed to her that any time conversation passed between them, he bested her. She therefore was determined to remain silent, saying as little as possible. But her silence seemed not to perturb him. While she continued to dig doggedly at the growing trench, Steve took out his flint and went to work on a fire. Soon a welcoming flame was leaping high, illuminating the darkness around them. Somewhere beyond the yellow circle of light a coyote yipped, and Steve's Appaloosa snorted an answer in return.

When she calculated the hole was long and deep enough, she collapsed before the fire, panting from her exertion. Steve untied the bag of supplies from the saddle horn and brought the bag over to the firelight. Squatting, he drew forth a small cast-iron skillet and a battered tin coffeepot.

"Here," he said, tossing her a pouch. "It's bacon slab. Slice us some while I start the coffee."

Victoria grimaced at him as he once more disappeared down the small slope with the coffeepot. Grudgingly she began slicing the bacon into the skillet. When Steve returned, he hunkered before the fire, mixing the ground coffee as expertly as any woman, and set the coffeepot, now filled with water, over the burning coals.

Aware that he watched her as she sliced the bacon, she rapidly finished and shoved the skillet over the small fire. Steve poured some coffee into an old tin cup and handed it to her. "You're not bad looking, *corazón*—for a *muchacho*."

"Let's hope you continue to consider me a boy."

"What? You haven't been pining away for my caresses?"

Victoria ignored his derisive smile. But she couldn't ignore the smelly, woolen poncho that covered most of her—or the baggy pants that she was continually hitching up about her waist. However, she had to admit that being dressed as a boy had probably saved her life. More than once she and Steve had encountered troops in their flight through the San Antonio streets.

The crisp aroma of frying bacon filled the air. "I'm hungry," she said, removing the floppy sombrero that covered her head and tossing it alongside the supply pack. Long pigtails fell out on her shoulders. She looked defiantly at Steve. "Or do I get to eat?"

"By all means. I plan to fatten you up," he said, taking the bacon from the skillet. "Can't stand to make love to a skinny woman."

Victoria refused to accept the barb but took the plate of fried bacon he held out to her. It was delicious, she thought, but refused to compliment Steve. Silently she ate, savoring the warmth of the fire and the food.

When they had finished, she immediately began cleaning up, not wanting to give Steve the opportunity to issue more orders. He, in turn, crossed to the Appaloosa where it stood grazing a little away from the makeshift camp. Victoria heard him say as he removed the saddle, "Easy, Guerrero. Just going to lighten your load."

He stroked the great beast with gentle motions, speaking gently to it in Spanish. Unable to restrain her curiosity Victoria asked, "Where did you learn Spanish?"

His face closed over. "From a Mexican girl the Comanches captured."

Victoria wanted to ask more, but the bronzed face in the firelight was formidable as he carried the saddle over to the trench, placing it on the north side of the elongated hole to act as a breaker against the wind. After he tossed some blankets alongside the hole, he settled back against the saddle and rolled a cigarette, his long fingers moving as skillfully as a professional card player's.

Refraining from questioning him further, Victoria finished putting everything away. Once again she was aware of those hawklike eyes watching her. Knowing that the time was drawing near for a confrontation, she looked up nervously. But Steve only said, in that peculiarly lazy drawl of his, "The stream's that way if you want to wash up," and jerked his head over his left shoulder.

"Thank you," she replied stiffly, leaving the shelter of the firelight and heading in the direction he had indicated.

It could not even be called a stream, so little water was there. She cupped her hands in its chilly surface and splashed a small amount on her face. It would not do much to wash away the grime and dust, but it revived her.

She turned and looked about her, her eyes straining in the darkness. But there was nothing but the whisper of the rising wind. Moving a little away to some clumps of brush, she fumbled awkwardly with the boy's pants she wore. Dropping them, she squatted and relieved the ache in her kidneys.

When she returned, her creamy complexion grew crimson with embarrassment realizing that Steve was probably well aware that she had been tending to her personal needs. But then, she rationalized, such things were natural to him, a man of the frontier, and he probably thought little of it.

She watched apprehensively as he rose and flipped the cigarette away, its tiny light arcing out into the darkness. "You ready to bed down, *corazón*?"

"Not with you."

One black brow lifted, but he only shrugged and said, "Suit yourself. It's going to get damn cold before morning comes."

He tossed her one of the Mexican blankets and stretched out his long frame in the trench. Indignantly she wrapped the blanket about her and lay down in front of the fire. However, it didn't take long, as Steve had so smugly predicted, before she realized she could not stay where she was much longer. Her front side was burning with the heat of the fire, and her backside was chilled to the bone. She stood it as long as she could. Some minutes later, when her teeth started chattering, she grabbed up her blanket and crossed to the trench.

With some uncanny sixth sense, it seemed to Victoria, Steve knew she was coming. She stood at the shallow hole's edge, and he held out one brown hand. "Been expecting you, Vicky."

"If you try anything, Steve Kaptain, I'll claw your eyes out—and your guts along with them." From beneath the poncho she withdrew the knife Steve had given her earlier to slice the bacon and brandished it over him.

Steve's laugh was harsh. "Do you think I've survived this many years out here out of carelessness? I watched you pocket the knife."

"Why—why didn't you do something?"

He took her wrist and pulled her down alongside him. "Will you shut up and get under the blanket. It's cold!" Pulling the blanket over them, he enclosed her in a cocoon of warmth.

She stiffened as he tried to pull her up against him, and moved away a few inches.

"Listen, Vicky," he said, jerking her up tightly against his own warm body, "I won't collect until I'm ready. And I'm certainly not in any mood tonight to jump your bones. Now go to sleep."

She squirmed, imprisoned within his arms, but his warmth soon enveloped her, and she quieted, falling asleep to the strong, steady beat of his heart.

She awoke to find his fathomless eyes watching her in the dim light of dawn. His head was propped on one hand, and in the other hand he held one of her pigtails, his long fingers toying with the feathery end.

She moved nervously, and he said, "I like your hair better loose—hanging down about your shoulders."

"You'll never see it that way."

"Don't make rash promises, Vicky." He stood up, and the early morning cold rushed in over her.

"Ohhh," she said, drawing the blankets up around her exposed body. "It's freezing!"

"Get up!" Steve ordered, yanking the blankets from her. "We've still got a long ride ahead of us."

She bounded to her feet, facing him with clenched hands. Hot fury boiled in her so that she did not feel the bite of the cold. "Steve Kaptain, I'm not your servant to be ordered . . ." but her voice fell away as the sage-green pupils of his eyes changed to the flat, deadly color of flint.

She had no doubt but that he would have no qualms about turning her in at the nearest town—or worse yet, selling her to the Comancheros, who, she had heard, carried on a profitable trade in captives, especially females.

Rebelliously, she whirled from him and began rolling the blankets. When all was packed, Steve mounted and held down his hand for her. She glared at him with all the hatred she felt and thought what a joy it would be to plunge her knife between his ribs. She slipped her foot in the stirrup and, accepting his hand, swung up behind him. But when she felt in her pants pocket for the knife, it was gone. Hastily she tried to remember when he had removed it from her.

"You took it," she accused to his back. "You took my knife!"

He continued to whistle some Spanish tune, one she recognized as *Rio Rebelde*. "Well, aren't you going to say anything?" she demanded.

"You'll get the knife back when I think you need it—and know how to use it properly."

At that moment she would have willingly become the murderess she was accused of being.

X

✼✼✼✼✼✼✼✼✼✼✼

Even as her hatred seethed within, Victoria was forced to huddle close to Steve. The chill March weather of northern Texas was like nothing she had experienced in either Reynosa or Vallejo.

By midafternoon a fine downpour of sleet moved out of the north, drenching the two of them. As the gray light of day began to fade, she felt she could take no more. "Steve!" she shouted above the whistle of the wind, "I'm a human icicle! Can't we stop?"

"It'd mean sure death," he shouted back over his shoulder. "Brandt's isn't much farther."

Half an hour later, fine flakes of snow began to fall

down on them like floating feathers, and Victoria wondered frantically if they could be lost. She was beginning to lose hope of surviving the unseasonable winter storm. She could not see how Steve knew where he was going with the blur of gray all about them. It was then she saw the trading post—a large cabin with an attached shed where several horses were already stabled.

As the Appaloosa approached with its two frozen riders, a man came out of the cabin. "Well, I'll be damned," Steve said, his breath rising like frosty smoke in the frigid air. "If it ain't Jake Dickey!"

The weatherbeaten man with the feathered hat took Guerrero's bridle while Steve dismounted. As the man's sad brown eyes took in herself and Steve, Victoria recognized him as the same taciturn man she had served whiskey to in Steve's room at Rose's.

"You're late," Jake said. "We was beginning to worry 'bout you."

"Had some other business to attend to, Jake."

Both of the men looked up at her, and she self-consciously slid out of the saddle into Steve's arms. He sat her down and said, "Didn't figure on meeting up with you till we crossed Mustang water hole."

"The news couldn't wait. King and Kenedy are ready to sell out now."

Engrossed in their conversation, the two men walked on ahead of Victoria as if she had never been there.

"That'll mean swinging by the ranch," Steve said, pushing open the cabin door. "With the sale of the cattle we should have enough cash."

Inside, Victoria paused, waiting for her eyes to adjust to the darkness. There was a feminine shriek. "Steven!" and Victoria perceived, running from the darkness of one corner, a young woman with slanted golden eyes and auburn hair curled atop her head in an elegant chignon. The woman threw herself into Steve's arms, emitting a deep, husky laugh.

"Maya," he said, finally releasing her, "who's buying your kisses now?"

"No one will ever buy my kisses. They're all yours, Steven."

Steve quirked one angled brow in sardonic amusement, and Maya said, "No, it's true, Steven. I've put my past behind me." She nodded toward a stout, swarthy man who sat in one corner cleaning his rifle and said, "Roberto has consented to let me drive one of his wagons in exchange for passage to El Paso."

"And then?" Steve asked.

Fierce passion blazed suddenly in Maya's eyes. "I've an aunt in El Paso . . . and I will wait there patiently for you, Steve. Until you move on. Then I will, too. I won't give you up."

There was an expression of loyalty and dedication in Maya's eyes that caught Victoria by surprise. Surprise also that the man Victoria detested so much could be capable of arousing such emotions as those blazing in Maya's eyes.

"You're quite a woman," Steve said. "Now get me some whiskey, baby."

"I'll get you more than that, Steve—later." She planted one last kiss on the long lips before relinquishing him to fetch the whiskey.

Behind Victoria Jake said, his voice low so that she could barely hear, "That's Roberto Duval in the corner, Steve. He wants to take several of his wagons to El Paso. Freighting merchandise to the people there

115

that can't get it. Tools and equipment and such. Neighbors said you might want to check Duval out. The rest get in tomorrow—if the weather holds out."

"Wondered if we were going to make it ourselves," Steve said. And then, as if suddenly remembering Victoria's presence, he nodded in her direction and said, "You recall this lovely young lady, don't you, Jake?"

A sympathetic smile touched Jake's mouth. "How you doing, Miss Romero?"

Victoria was astonished that Jake recognized her in the boy's clothing, for Maya, she knew, had not. "I'm fine, thank you, Jake," she replied. But she was far from feeling it. She still shook with cold, and after Maya's blatant sensuality, she could only feel disgust as she glanced down at her sodden britches and dirt-smeared poncho. She knew she must look awful.

As if reading her thoughts, Steve said, "Go sit by the fire, Vicky. You'll feel better after you've had a chance to warm up."

It was one order Victoria willingly followed. She passed a counter behind which was stocked provisions that supplied the settlements there on the Brazos River and the few military families that occupied the crude stockade of Fort Spunky.

At the far end of the counter was a row of pegs on which were hung a saber, forage cap, and uniform. Ridding herself of the sombrero and smelly poncho, Victoria hung them on one of the pegs before crossing to the hearth.

Gratefully she slid into the pine rocker set before the crackling fire and tried to remove the heavy boots Steve had found for her. But each time she jarred her foot, pain shot up her leg. Several times more she tried to get the boot off, but the sticky wet leather adhered to her foot.

She bit her lower lip in agonized determination, and Jake, seeing the look of pain etched on her face, came over and knelt at her side. "Here, missy, let me help."

Taking hold of her leg above the boot with one hand, he squeezed, slowing the flow of blood to her foot. With the other hand he gently began to work the boot off. Victoria looked down at her foot and saw purple-ridged veins extended in her cold, blue-white skin.

"Steve," Jake called.

Steve left off rolling his cigarette and took the whiskey bottle Maya handed him. Even from the other side of the room Victoria could see Maya's enrapt face, her golden eyes speaking eloquently of passion. Grimacing, she turned back as Jake took hold of her other leg and applied pressure.

"What is it?" Steve asked, coming over and squatting on his haunches before Jake and Victoria.

Jake pointed at her feet. "Could be frostbite."

"Here," Steve said, handing her the bottle. "Drink this."

She shook her head. "I don't like it."

"I said drink it, Vicky."

His eyes narrowed, and she glared back. "You're—you're—"

Jake rose and spat a stream of tobacco juice into a spittoon on the hearth. "Better go out and look for Brandt," he said. "He's supposed to be rounding up the livestock, but this weather could give him some trouble."

"I know," Steve told Victoria when Jake tactfully

departed, "I'm detestable and you hate me. I'm getting tired of hearing it."

He put the bottle to her lips before she could protest further and poured the fiery liquid in her mouth. She choked and sputtered.

"My little *muchacho*," Steve laughed softly. "I could be thrown in the poke for giving liquor to a little boy."

"I told you, Steve Kaptain, I'm not yours!" Angrily she pushed the bottle away from her mouth.

Steve smiled and set the bottle down. "The way you look now, *corazón*, I don't think I'd want you."

"That suits me just fine."

"Good! Perhaps I'll turn you over to the Karanka-was." He picked up her swollen foot and began rubbing it briskly with his warm hands. "Doubt they'd want you either," he continued. "They're cannibals, you know. And your flesh doesn't look particularly appetizing right now. 'Course," he said, as she sat stubbornly silent, "after the circulation gets going you might not be a bad piece of merchandise."

The touch of his fingers against the soft skin of her foot stirred something inside her. Harshly, she said, "I don't believe you."

Steve stopped and shot her a piercing look. "Don't ever make the mistake of taking what I say lightly, Vicky."

Maya came over, her long red skirts sashaying about her ankles. At once she recognized Victoria, and her eyes flashed murderously when she saw the small foot cradled in Steve's hands. "Is she going, too?"

Steve looked up at Victoria, his eyes inscrutable. "It appears so," he said slowly.

"She doesn't have to go," Maya pressed. "You could

say no. You're the one that's going to lead the party to El Paso."

"I'm sharing that dubious honor," Steve said, putting Victoria's foot down and picking up the other, "with Lieutenant Garrett."

"Ted Garrett?" Victoria asked.

Steve paused in his rubbing and looked up at her. "Do you know him?"

"I met him—some time ago," she answered evasively.

"Maya," Steve said, rising, "get some dry clothing from behind the counter for Victoria."

Maya looked down at her, her lip curling disdainfully. "You look like a drowned rat," she said, for the first time addressing Victoria.

"Your opinion matters little to me," Victoria replied coolly.

Maya whirled back to Steve. "Why did you bring her here, Steven?"

"Damned if I know," he muttered, and stalked off, leaving the two young women facing each other like bristling cats.

XI

✚✚✚✚✚✚✚✚✚✚✚✚

Unwillingly, Victoria shared the double bed in the back room of the trading post that night with Maya, while the men slept on the floor about the fireplace.

While Victoria took off the baggy pants, with only the long cotton shirt to cover her torso, Maya stripped with brazen deliberation. Removing her skirt and blouse, she stood before Victoria clad·only in her shift. Her voluptuous breasts strained against the thin cotton. She put her hands on her hips and smiled scornfully.

"You're nothing but a scrawny little girl, Victoria. It was stupid to be jealous of you—even for a moment. You could mean nothing to Steve. You're not his type.

He likes . . ." Maya's eyes roamed over Victoria's petite frame with ridicule. "his women to look like women."

Victoria's eyes froze into chips of blue ice, but she replied calmly, "Then I thank you for the compliment, Maya."

Maya's eyes narrowed with suspicion.

"Because," Victoria went on, "Steve's type of woman is only one kind—*la puta*. And a prostitute is what you always have been and always will be."

"I'll claw your eyes out for that!" Maya lunged at Victoria, but the smaller girl lithely dodged.

"Wait," Victoria said, holding up a hand to halt the other woman and laughing outright.

Hatred contorted Maya's sensuous face. "And what is so funny?"

"We are. We're fighting like two alley cats for no reason. Listen, Maya. I find Steve Kaptain rude and detestable. I don't want him! Do you understand? The man's yours. I couldn't be more happy that you want him. That way you'll keep him away from me!"

Maya looked at Victoria with disbelief, but said finally, "Perhaps you are telling the truth. But I'll remind you to also keep away from him. Do *you* understand?"

"Quite." Ignoring the truculent glare in the other woman's eyes, Victoria crawled into the bed and fell asleep immediately.

She rose earlier than Maya and donned a brown skirt and white cotton peasant blouse that were among the clothing Maya had gathered for her from Brandt's provision the night before. Not only did the low-cut blouse expose more of herself than she liked, but both the blouse and skirt hung on her smaller frame like clothes on a scarecrow. With her braids hanging over her shoulders, Victoria thought she looked like a reservation squaw.

In the main room some of the men had already awakened, stretching and yawning like great bears. Nowhere did Victoria see Steve. But there were three more men in the room than had been there when she had retired the previous night. One of them, a skinny man with a hook-shaped nose, stirred the coals in the fireplace. He was vaguely familiar to Victoria.

She crossed the room and began searching for coffee, when a heavy-set man with a balding head appeared at her side. "Looking for something?" he asked gruffly.

Victoria looked up at the close-set eyes. "I thought the men would like some coffee."

"Brandt's my name. You'll find the coffee in that box behind you. There in the cupboard."

"I do believe it's the beautiful young lady from San Antonio," a voice said from behind them.

Victoria turned, trembling, to face Rip Ford. She knew that if he was aware of the murder charges against her all hope was gone. She could only brazen it out. "Rip, how pleasant to see you again. Did you just arrive from San Antonio also?"

"Austin. Neighbors and I brought in several wagonloads more of people this morning—all of them hoping to make a new start out west." His warm eyes swept over her with interest. "Is that true of you, too?"

"You might say that," she said vaguely, but inwardly she breathed a sigh of relief. Ford could not possibly yet know of Antonio Morales's murder if he had been in Austin.

A man of medium stature with an open face approached them, forestalling further questioning by Rip. "Neighbors," Rip said, "I want you to meet the young lady who's practically charmed all of San Antonio, Miss Victoria Romero. Victoria, Major Robert Neighbors."

"My pleasure, ma'am," Neighbors said, tipping his hat over his friendly gray eyes. "And a disappointment, I might add, that we won't be going all the way to El Paso with you."

"Oh? I was under the impression that both of you, along with Mr. Kaptain, were to lead the wagon train."

Neighbors glanced at Rip. "That was true, Miss Romero," the major answered, sweeping his straight brown hair back over his head and putting on his hat again. "But we've had some difficulties with Mexican raiders at Rio Grande City. General Woolf has ordered us to leave the wagon train at Snake Springs."

"Lieutenant Garrett," Rip said, "and a few soldiers at Fort McKavett will replace us."

Victoria wanted to inquire further of Ted Garrett, but someone called out for coffee and she was forced to make her excuses to Rip and Neighbors.

All at once the trading post was astir. Victoria paused only once more in the next half hour, in the midst of mixing biscuit dough, when Steve came in, his snow-covered hat pulled low over his eyes. In his arms was a load of firewood. After he got a roaring blaze going, he joined Ford and Neighbors and some of the other men who had settled themselves around the wooden, oblong table to discuss the journey.

Victoria wondered with apprehension if Steve would divulge to the other two men the reason for her inclusion in the wagon train. Steve was so unpredictable, a man whose actions did not coincide with the ordinary habits of other men, that she found it hard to judge what he would do.

Maya finally awoke and petulantly helped Victoria serve the breakfast. As the sloe-eyed creole set a plate before Steve, he wrapped an arm about her waist even as he continued in his conversation with the proprietor, Brandt. Irritated at Steve's presumptuous manner with women, Victoria unknowingly slammed a cup down in front of Neighbors, sloshing the coffee, and the major looked up in surprise. Steve's penetrating gaze switched to Victoria, and she mumbled an apology before hurrying away.

After breakfast, Victoria was putting away the dishes when Steve came up behind her. "Then you can be domestic, *corazón*. Not just another pretty face."

An image of herself as a squaw that morning flashed through her mind, and she had to laugh in spite of herself. She put the dish towel down and turned around. "That's one statement of yours I'll have to take lightly," she said, smiling.

The long eyes narrowed in surprise that mingled with curiosity, and Victoria nervously pushed back a stray tendril that had escaped her tight braiding. "Did —did you want something?"

"Ever driven a wagon before?"

"No. Why?"

"Then come," he said, taking her wrist. "You're going to learn in one short, easy course."

She grabbed up the poncho, finally dry, from one of

the pegs as Steve pulled her to the door. Outside, the yard was filled with men, women, and children. And wagons and pack mules as far as her eye could see. Like she had been, the women were busy cleaning up after breakfast over open fires, while the men were making the last-minute preparations for the trek.

Steve led her over to a wagon by itself. "I chose this one for you," he said, lifting her up into the seat. "Sturdy axles and wheels and a good team of horses."

"Steve, it'll take me forever to repay you," she said, dismayed.

There was a cynical twist to his smile. "I told you, you'll work it out. Besides, *corazón*, the wagon isn't all yours." He jerked his head toward the rear of the wagon. "There's a load of Sharps rifles that Brandt wants to sell to the people at San Elizario, near El Paso. I take the wagon for him, and your passage and supplies are paid."

"And, I assume, you get a share of the profits?"

"You don't think I'm risking my neck solely to get you out of the area, do you, Vicky? Don't attribute any high motives to my actions."

"I assure you, Mr. Kaptain, I've no illusions about you."

He chuckled and flicked the reins lightly. "Now watch—and listen to what I tell you."

He was as proficient at maneuvering the wagon as he was at handling a horse . . . or a woman, Victoria thought, for he was surprisingly and infinitely patient with her initially unwieldy movements as she tried to control the team.

By noon, when the wagon train was packed and ready to set out, the sun had burned off the clouds and driven away the cold, so that it was a fine spring afternoon with only the patches of melting snow covering the ground to remind them of winter's late presence.

Steve gave the order of formation to each teamster, placing Victoria in the middle. Three wagons behind her were the Duval wagons, with Maya occupying one and Roberto the other. At the rear of the train Jake rode. And all about were small herds of goats and pigs and cattle, and every so often a milk cow tethered to the rear of a wagon like a family pet.

In all, eighteen wagons set out in a northwesterly direction following the Leon River to Antelope Creek, where they would make their first camp. Steve had told her the wagons covered as little as three miles an hour, fifteen to forty miles a day, depending on the distance between water holes, and that it could take as long as six weeks to reach El Paso.

If she reached there at all, Victoria thought. For she was still determined to escape Steve at some point, though her conscience nagged her that some sort of payment was in order in spite of the treatment she had received at his hands.

With misgivings, Victoria started up her wagon along with the others. Despite Steve's instructions, she was terrified to be responsible for the four large mules yoked to the harness of her wagon; but she refused to let Steve see her fear, knowing it would give him just one more thing to ridicule her about.

But nothing serious happened that first day. Once the two lead mules shied when a couple of prairie dogs popped suddenly from their ground holes. Several times during the afternoon Steve, sometimes with Rip or Neighbors at his side, rode back to check the wagons. But, although he never came alongside Victoria's, she knew those keen sage-green eyes took in everything.

That evening the wagons camped on the banks of the Leon beneath a grove of sycamores. Steve positioned the wagons in a horseshoe with an opening of about twenty-five feet to enable the animals to be driven inside the corral in case of an alarm. Some of the men he assigned as cattle guards, and others the task of getting wood or dried buffalo chips for fuel, and still others the job of kindling the fires. The women's job was to devote themselves to the preparation of the evening's meal.

It was Victoria's first opportunity to get acquainted with the other women passengers. None seemed to think it unusual that she was traveling alone. For each of them were unusual in their own right, leaving the security of their own homes and relatives for the unknown.

Viola Bentley, a stringbean of a woman, beaten down by years on the frontier, became Victoria's first friend in the wagon train. She showed Victoria where the buckets and lanterns were hung beneath the wagon beds and helped her unload the mess chest. The scrawny woman was pregnant, and she held her protruding stomach gently as the two women set the chests in the buffalo grass.

"Are you all right, Viola?"

Viola nodded, a smile creasing her brown, weatherlined face. "Yep, I'm doing just fine, honey. My man, Jess, he says I'm getting too old to have another one. Mayhaps he's right. Thirty-six is getting up there in years."

"Then you have other children?"

Viola put her hand over her eyes as if to shield off the glare of the dying sun and looked across the Leon. "No, honey," she said in a tight voice, "there's been four others. Tiny little mites that jest didn't seem to wanna live. Jess and me, we thought about starting over somewhere new like. Mayhaps this time . . ." She let her voice trail off.

Victoria put her hand on the older woman's arm. "I've heard that El Paso is a beautiful town ringed by mountains. I'm sure you'll have a beautiful baby to match the town."

"Well, honey, we got to get ourselves there first. And this chawing ain't gon'na get it done. Come on, girl. Let's get started."

Victoria also met another young girl, Judith, who had only recently married. She and her husband, Billy Lee, a serious youth with wheat-colored hair, had left Tennessee in hopes of finding a better life. Proudly, she showed Victoria her treasure chest, filled with wedding gifts. Beautifully quilted blankets, home-made rugs, embroidered sheets and pillow cases—and even a set of fine china.

"Is your husband out hunting game with the others," the girl asked shyly, "or has he been posted here?"

"I—I'm not married, Judith." Using Maya's aunt as a reason, Victoria said, "I'm traveling to El Paso to stay with relatives there." Victoria looked away uncomfortably, hating the lie.

"Well, as pretty as you are," the redheaded girl said, mistaking Victoria's discomposure for embarrassment at not being already married, "you'll soon have yourself a man. I hear there's not enough women in the

West. And that men even pay for their brides like they would items in those mail-order catalogues. Why I bet we could even find you a husband right here on the wagon train."

Victoria smiled at the young girl's naïve attempt at matchmaking. "A husband is the last thing I want, Judith."

The women had everything set up by the time the men returned packing several wild turkeys. The dinner was served with beans and hard bread, and Victoria sat around one of the campfires that included an older couple in their sixties, the Towerses, who seemed determined to take her in like they would have their own daughter.

Sim Towers, who clicked his teeth like castanets when he talked, explained to Victoria that they had lost their crops to hordes of grasshoppers and as a result lost their farm to the bank.

His wife Amy patted his veined hand consolingly. Her wrinkled face, with the pepper and salt hair smoothed tidily back in a bun, radiated boundless affection for him. "It's going to be all right, Sim, sweet. We'll build ourselves a bigger and better nest in El Paso."

Victoria could not help but admire the venerable couple for their courage and their obvious love for one another. If Victoria thought she could find a man to love like that, to share both the hardships and the joys of life, she told herself she would marry without hesitation.

With more than fifty people to feed, it was well past dark before everything was cleaned and packed away. Most of the families had bedded down beneath their own wagons, and a few of the men still milled about the fire where the whispers of gold and California could be heard from those who were only using El Paso as a stopover.

It was the moment Victoria had been waiting for. As the evening's hush descended on the camp, she went in search of Steve.

XII

✠✠✠✠✠✠✠✠✠✠✠

It was one of those perfect spring nights. The silvered moon was high and the night air crisp. Crickets and frogs harmonized in a serenade to the night's starry beauty.

Victoria found Steve off to himself, squatting on the banks of the river and watching the distant horizon as if something were out there. A tin cup of steaming coffee he held between his hands.

She thought she had come upon him quietly, but, without turning his head, he said, "You should be asleep, Vicky."

"How did you know it was me?" She stood beside him, afraid almost to take a seat.

"By the rhythm of your steps." He looked up at her, and the mischievous smile that played about the mobile lips made him look years younger. "And by your smell."

"I washed up this morning!"

"That may be, but every living thing has a particular odor. The pack mule over by that nearest wagon, for instance, has an entirely different odor than the tethered horses or grazing cattle."

Intrigued and forgetting her nervousness, she sat down a few inches away from Steve. "And what is my odor?"

"Oh, somewhere between a mixture of woodsmoke and lavender, orange blossoms and musk."

She looked up to see if he was teasing, but his roughly planed face was quite serious. "How did you learn all this—about hunting and smells and trapping?"

"I was a captive for two years with the Kiowas. Up along the Trinity River. When I was twelve, I escaped."

He said it so flatly, Victoria knew that it had to have been a painful memory. "Did you return to your parents?"

"There was nothing to return to. My family was killed at the same time as I was taken captive."

"You—you don't hate them—the Indians?"

"Would it do any good? We've done the same or worse to them."

"What happened after you escaped?"

"Jake found me. He had been trailing the band I

was a prisoner with. His daughter was captured shortly after I was."

Intuition made Victoria ask, "The girl you learned Spanish from?"

"Yes. Jake's wife was Mexican. She died in childbirth, and when his only child, Isabel, was taken captive on her thirteenth birthday, Jake set out to find her. But our band was a nomadic one, and it was almost two years before he caught up with us. During that time an old Kiowa decided he wanted to take Isabel as his bride. She didn't survive the year."

Victoria did not know what to say. True, she had experienced the same as Isabel must have. But only once, not repeatedly. She shivered with the memory.

"That same year," Steve continued, "I made my escape. Jake saved me from near-starvation and exhaustion. And in these past twenty years, he still thinks I need watching over, just as if I were twelve again."

"And since then?"

"The Texas Rangers hired me on as a scout for the Mexican-American War."

"Yes, I know," she said, unable to halt the bitterness that seeped into her voice like swamp water.

Steve's eyes searched her face, and she turned away, disturbed by their relentless scrutiny.

"I came to ask you about Ford," she said, changing the subject. "He knows where I'm going, who I am. What happens when he finally learns of the order for my arrest. Am I in danger of being reported?"

Steve tossed out the remainder of his coffee. "I think Rip has too high an opinion of you to do something like that."

"But still," she persisted, "someone could slip up. Accidentally say something about having seen me."

"It doesn't make any difference," Steve said, getting to his feet. "I took care of that before we left San Antone." He held out one strong hand and, after a brief moment, she placed her own in it, letting him pull her up beside him.

"What do you mean?"

"Enrique and I had a private talk. He agreed, under a small amount of pressure, to have the murder charges withdrawn."

Victoria should have been relieved, but she wasn't. "You mean—you mean, I've come all this way—gone through all this—for nothing?"

His lips parted in a half-smile, revealing the even, white teeth. "And you've been a real trooper about it, *corazón*. Never once complained about the hardships."

"Ohh," she said, in a half-sigh, half-hiss.

Steve encircled her waist with one muscle-corded arm. "What would you have done had you known, Vicky?" he whispered in her ear. "Where would you have gone?"

She stood there, trembling with fury . . . and something else, as Steve's lips began to roam about her face, softly brushing her skin like the touch of butterfly wings.

"Besides," he added, "I needed someone to drive the wagonload of rifles."

She broke from his embrace. "You—you've been using me all along!" Her blue eyes burned purple in their depths. "I swear I'll—"

Steve took her by the shoulders and pulled her to

136

him. "Remember, I told you not to make promises you can't—"

"Steve!" It was Jake's voice.

Steve released Victoria abruptly, and she almost slumped to the ground.

"There's a party of Comanches back in camp. Yellow Wolf wants to do some talking—and trading, I suspect. Got their eyes on our horses."

"I know. Been following their movements out there. They've been watching us for over an hour." He turned to Victoria. "Go to your wagon," he told her and strode off with Jake before she could protest.

All her life she had heard how savage the Indians were, and her stomach sucked in with nervous terror. Still, her curiosity was greater, and she followed Steve and Jake at a distance back into the camp where she could watch what went on.

There were five of them. They were tall, and in the firelight, their skin was cinnamon-colored, glistening with the oil rubbed into their bodies. Behind the five men were three women bearing hide packs on their backs.

Viola and Maya came up behind Victoria. "What do you think they want, Viola?" Victoria whispered.

"It ain't good, whatever it is. Never trust them demons."

Victoria watched one of the Indians who seemed to be doing all the negotiating and wondered if he was Yellow Wolf. He wore a breechcloth and knee-high buckskin moccasins. Lank, long black hair was held back from his oblique eyes by a band of red flannel.

"What's he saying?" Maya asked.

"*Cha-ta*," Viola replied. "It means good. I think he's

telling Mr. Kaptain the tobacco is good. In a few minutes he'll get down to the business that brought them here."

Jess, a tall, gangling man with thinning red hair, joined the women, placing a protective arm about Viola's bony shoulders. "They probably want to trade them packs those squaws are a-carrying for a horse or two," her husband said.

"That's damn stupid, I say!" It was Roberto Duval's barrel-chested voice. "Letting those stinking renegades come into our camp. Ought to shoot every last one of them. Teach those others out there not to mess around with us."

"Shut your trap, man," Viola said. "You wanna get them riled? Mr. Kaptain knows what he's a-doing."

Steve motioned to the Indians to follow him, and he and Jake, along with Rip and Neighbors, returned to the campfire; they squatted around it, waiting for the Indians to join them. Silently, one of the Comanches took a long, thin reed, much like a pipe, and held it to his mouth, inhaling. This was then passed to the next one in the circle about the fire. When each had had their turn, the talk began.

At one point, the three Indian women untied the rawhide-bound packs and brought out pelts. Even from where Victoria stood, she could see fur was deep and luxurious.

One of the Indian women was young, perhaps no more than fifteen or sixteen, but already with a womanly, curved figure, and Victoria watched as she passed some of the pelts around for each man to examine. She paused in front of Steve longer than the others, her dark and sensuous eyes obviously beseeching his attentions.

He seemed not to notice but nodded, saying something, before turning his attention to the next woman who exhibited her pelts for him. This went on for thirty minutes more before one of the chieftains, the one thought to be Yellow Wolf, signaled that the parley was over. Everyone came to their feet then, but the men from the wagon train remained where they were, while Steve, deep in conversation with Yellow Wolf, followed the Comanches to the edge of camp. They halted there, as if waiting, and then Jake appeared with Steve's horse.

"Where's he going, Viola?" Victoria asked.

"Not sure I followed everything," Viola said. " 'Pears he's going back to their camp to do some more talking. Most likely 'bout getting Yellow Wolf to help him find two Penatoka Comanche guides he's looking for."

After the tension that had slowly mounted, the spectators turned away, seeking their wagons—relieved and somewhat disappointed at the same time.

Victoria had only the front half of her wagon to serve as sleeping quarters, since the rear was packed with rifles. Around the inside of the wagon were hung the things that would be needed on the journey—pots and pans, towels, clothing, and blankets. It was well past midnight, and a chill had crept into the night air, so Victoria, spreading out a blanket on the bottom of the wagon, made her bed inside.

She was not as cramped for space as she had thought she would be, but had she the whole wagon to stretch out in, she could not have slept. The night was filled with noises, and once, when one of the camp dogs howled at the moon, Victoria sat up with fright.

She looked out from her wagon and saw many forms stretched out on the ground, using their saddles as pillows, but she did not recognize any of them as belonging to Steve. Nor was his Appaloosa, Guerrero, tethered with the other horses.

It had been a restless night for Victoria, and as she bent over the river bank to wash up, she saw the shadows beneath her eyes, intensifying their cool blueness. She rose from her kneeling position and was drying her face when she saw Steve crossing the Leon from the opposite bank, his horse swimming in the water halfway up its flanks.

She knew then where Steve had spent the night. Probably, she thought scornfully, with the Indian girl who had such inviting eyes. Victoria had no doubt but that Steve took the girl just as carelessly and arrogantly as he had taken her. Her anger flared at the memory, and she went about the camp that morning with compressed lips and tight movements. Like dynamite and flame, all she needed, she thought exasperatedly, was one sharp word to set off an explosion within her.

She could feel Steve's eyes on her, the curiosity burning there in their green depths, but she refused to meet the questioning gaze. She was in the wagon, packing the provisions, when he climbed aboard, pulling aside the canvas flaps to come inside.

"Okay, Vicky. What's got your fur standing on end?" He squatted there, the two of them enclosed in the wagon's cavelike darkness, and drew forth a thin piece of paper. He watched her through half-closed lids as he sprinkled the tobacco from his pouch on the paper and rolled it between thumb and forefinger.

"Well?"

"Where were you last night? Suppose those—those Comanches had attacked? How was I suppose to defend myself?" She flung out her hand. "These rifles of yours are worthless without bullets!"

"Are you finished?" He lit up the cigarette, its light illuminating their faces.

"Yes!"

"I didn't leave you unprotected, Vicky. Jake had instructions to take care of you—and he also has the ammunition for the rifles—should you become desperate. Anything else?"

"You still didn't tell me what you were doing?" she said, exasperated by his calm reasoning.

"Do you really want to know?"

They were so close to each other, she could smell the tobacco on his husky-voiced words. She turned her head away. "No."

"So you're the haughty *hidalgo* again? When your stiff-necked pride burns itself out, you might try this on. I get mighty tired of seeing you look like a border-town whore."

"Ohhh," she said, *"quién pensas eres—"* but he had already gone, his soft laughter following his light footsteps.

Before her was the object he had left, carefully folded. Hesitantly, she reached out and picked it up. From within the folds a pair of moccasins with the high leather leggings fell out. But her attention was held by the dress. It was of soft, tanned hide with intricate designs of hand-sewn beads.

141

Almost with reverence she held it against her, wishing desperately for a mirror. But she could tell it would fit exactly, its hem falling just below her knees.

She had not received such a wondrous gift since she was a child, before the death of her parents, and she blinked back the tears that welled in her eyes. Her childhood fantasies of fairies and leprechauns had never completely died, and she laughed to herself, for it was impossible for her to think of Steve as some leprechaun—much less the Prince Charming who always loved the princess, setting her high on a pedestal.

The sting of his parting retort did not dim her joy as she stripped off her dust-encrusted clothes and pulled the dress over her head. It hugged her small waist and curving hips as if it had been made especially for her.

Stepping out into the morning sunlight, her eyes searched for Steve. She knew it would be difficult, but she wanted to thank him. He could be thoughtful when he wanted to.

Maya, coming from the river with a pail of water in both hands, stopped and looked at Victoria with large golden eyes that narrowed with malice. Her carmine lips curled spitefully. "So, Steven sleeps with the pretty little Indian girl—and you get her dress. Not a bad exchange for his services."

Victoria turned on her with clenched hands. "Shut up!"

Maya laughed huskily, thinking all the while how glad she was Steven had finally tired of the small spitfire and turned his attentions elsewhere. She promised herself the opportunity would soon come for her to capture the heart of Steven. Having shared his embraces, Maya knew she could never be satisfied with less than his love.

Victoria watched in silent anger as Maya continued on her way to the wagon.

"What's ailing you, Victoria child?"

Victoria turned to Viola, clad as always in her cheap calico dress and heavy shoes. "It's Steve Kaptain, Viola. He's nothing but a hired gunfighter, a drifter, a—a *bastardo*!"

Dear Lord, it was bad enough for him to make love to one woman and in the same day give her a gift—but for the gift to have been the other woman's dress—that took sheer arrogance! She felt at that moment she could have torn the dress off in shreds had there not been others around.

"Why, honey," Viola said, taking Victoria's hand between her own red, callused hands, "I do believe you care about that man."

"That's ridiculous!" Victoria turned and stalked back to the wagon. Viola followed her. "He's nothing but a worthless drifter," Victoria muttered bitterly.

Both of the women halted at the wagon and watched Steve give directions to the men. "That's not what I see," Viola said, "when I look at him. He's one fine man in my books, honey."

Victoria looked at the woman with surprise before her eyes again sought out Steve, taller than those around him. "Yes, I guess you could call him handsome in a rugged sort of way . . . if you have a lot of imagination."

XIII

✻✻✻✻✻✻✻✻✻✻✻

Victoria found that each morning the time spent in getting packed was an experience in itself. Mess chests, sheet-iron kettles, canvas, and a hundred other items had to be packed on the mules. Since there were two or three dozen mules, this took several hours at the outset of each day's march; so that the first packed mule would grow tired of standing and usually broke and ran—sometimes bucking or rolling until it managed to scatter its burden. And the whole process would begin again.

Despite her irritation at being tricked into the journey west, she had to admit to herself that she was enjoying the trek immensely—the people, the adventure, the challenge. Only the weather failed to bring delight. For two days after the wagons left the first encampment the skies poured down a sea of rain. Many of the wagons had rotted canvas covers that were like sieves when the rains came. The wagon Steve had procured for Victoria was not only snug and tight against the elements, but, because of the extra wide rims on the wagon's wheels, it avoided being mired in the mud that bogged down some of the other wagons.

During this time Steve was preoccupied with the slow progress of the wagon train, and Victoria was spared his taunting eyes and derisive lips. Although once or twice a day she would see him ride by on Guerrero, his sharp eyes going over her wagon, checking it out, as he passed by to inspect the others.

On the fourth day of the journey the wagons arrived at Old Owl's camp on the Armstrong Creek. Here, Neighbors had told Victoria, in the camp of the Penatoka Comanches, Yellow Wolf promised to find the guides Steve was seeking for the wagon train, guides who would be able to aid Steve in finding the best passable route for the wagons to travel to El Paso.

The wagon camp was set up on the opposite bank of the Comanche camp. As the men went about the duties assigned to them, the women and children slipped down to the creek bank to gaze in fascination at the sights on the other side.

None of the pioneers had ever seen so many Indians at one time—over five thousand. And as far as the eye could see were large, conical-shaped huts that were thatched with long grass so that to Victoria they resembled haystacks at a distance. The Comanche children were everywhere—bathing in the creek, beating the bushes and thickets for snakes and rabbits, and the older ones riding the ponies in imitation of their fathers.

Victoria was among those watching from the bank along with Judith and Amy and Sim Towers. On Victoria's right was Elizabeth Caldwell and her two-year-old son Jason. The woman, who wore a perpetually dissatisfied frown on her painted face, Victoria found hard to get to know. She spoke little, and then only in complaints.

But Victoria felt pity stir in her for the woman when old Amy, who acted more like a bride with her Sim than Judith with Billy Lee, explained that the woman's husband had fallen off the roof of their barn and killed himself. Elizabeth Caldwell, Amy said, had been forced to accept the offer of her brother to come west with his family.

If Elizabeth was difficult to get to know, the child Jason was not. With blond, sun-streaked curls, apple cheeks, and large brown eyes shadowed by incredibly long lashes, Jason appealed to Victoria's latent maternal instincts.

So it was naturally she who first noticed that Jason had wandered off. She spotted his small form farther along the bank just as he stepped from the shallow part of the creek, apparently heading for the Indian children on the opposite bank, into the deeper part where he rapidly sank from view.

Without thinking, Victoria plunged into the water. With her heavy skirts, she found it hard to keep her balance and was swept forward by the current. Jason's little body was bobbing just ahead of her but, though she tried to wade to him, the current, stronger than usual due to the spring rains, kept him just out of her reach.

Above the screaming from the people on the bank she heard Steve shout, "Grab hold!"

She looked around in time to catch one end of the rawhide riata he tossed her. Rapidly he wrapped the other end about the saddle horn. Spurring his horse forward, he proceeded deeper into the stream, dragging Victoria behind him.

The next thing she knew, when she was able to blink the muddy water from her eyes, was that Steve held the child cradled in one arm while he reined Guerrero back toward the bank.

Victoria managed to straggle ashore as Steve returned Jason, who pulled happily at the frontiersman's bright red handkerchief, to the weeping Elizabeth. In her relief, the mother hurried away with the soaked toddler, forgetting to thank either Steve or Victoria.

Steve turned on Victoria, his voice sharp. "Hell's fires, Vicky! Don't you have enough sense to remove those damn skirts before pulling a stunt like that?"

Hair lay plastered to Victoria's face like seaweed, and she wrapped her arms about herself to still her trembling. "What was I supposed to do?" she asked, between spasmodic gasps. "Strip naked while Jason floated away?"

Steve's voice was clipped and cold. "If you had drowned, would it have saved the boy?"

He wheeled Guerrero about, leaving Victoria standing there numbed with shock and cold. Judith, Viola, and Amy crowded around her, trying to offer some comfort, when Rip edged his way through the women.

"Here," he said, wrapping a wool blanket about her. "We don't need a pneumonia patient on our hands."

She managed to return his warm smile as he led her back to the encircled wagons. "I'll never understand that man," she muttered furiously.

Rip laughed. "I think he's probably saying the same thing about you right now, Victoria."

At dawn that morning Buffalo Hump and Tall Tree rode into the wagon camp. The sleepy eyes of the pioneers opened wide upon seeing the two guides. Buffalo Hump, short and stout, unlike most of his tribe, scorned European clothing. His upper body was naked, and he wore a buffalo hide around his ample hips. Brass rings encircled his arms, and a string of beads hung about his neck. His serious, apathetic eyes swept over the pioneers before he turned away to seek out Steve.

But Tall Tree squatted before one of the campfires impassively while the people went uneasily about their work. In his own way, Tall Tree was just as impressive as Buffalo Hump. From the rear no one would have known him to be an Indian. He wore a dark, stylish cloth coat from a San Antonio haberdashery and a black semimilitary oilcloth cap. But from the front his dull, bestial expression betrayed him.

At the cracking of the whips and Steve's command to "Stretch out," the wagons fell into place and began the march. Traveling in a southwesterly direction, they reached the camp of Sanaco, the chieftain of a small band of the Penatokas, the following day. There the wagon train had its first experience with their colorful guide, Buffalo Hump. Early the next morning, before dawn had even lightened the skies, the pioneers were awakened by the screeching notes of what sounded like a song.

Her hair tumbled about her shoulders, Victoria looked out between the canvas flaps of the wagon. Steve, who always slept nearby, was already up and rolling his blanket. "What was that?" she asked.

In the predawn darkness she could not see his face, but she heard him chuckle. "That's something between the calling of hogs, the bellowing of a small bull, and the croaking of a solitary bull frog. That's Buffalo Hump's serenade to the new day."

The camp was to discover that they were to be treated to this serenade every morning for the next five mornings, when, to their relief, Buffalo Hump suddenly and mysteriously disappeared. When Victoria questioned Neighbors about it, the major's usually friendly face grew austere.

"Buffalo Hump found out that Ford and myself were leaving and 'd be replaced by Garrett. And, well, ma'am, I just don't guess he cottoned to the idea."

Victoria sensed there were underlying implications, but she left it at that, feeling it was none of her business.

Rolling due west over gently undulating country that had an abundant supply of water, timber, and grass, the wagon train reached Snake Springs late one evening. It was a day the pioneers had been looking forward to since leaving Brandt's trading post almost two weeks earlier. Here, instead of rising early in the morning and setting off for the next supply of water, Mustang water hole, they would lay over a day, waiting for the arrival of Rip and Neighbors' replacement, Ted Garrett.

The women were already planning a party in celebration. The following morning the entire female population of the wagon train could be found at the springs washing out dirty clothes while the men went hunting in preparation for the feast to be held that evening. Taking the respite from the male presence, the women bathed and washed their hair, laughing like little girls.

The men in the wagon train who had not gone out to hunt set up the encampment for the fiesta that night. Benches were quickly constructed which were set out to make a square, and lanterns were strung from the trees.

In anticipation of seeing Ted again, Victoria spent the afternoon taking in a summery cotton dress that was much too large. But it was almost pure white, and she knew that against the blue-blackness of her hair, the rather plain dress would be quite lovely.

During those hours she tried to analyze her thoughts, but they were too jumbled. She knew that she perhaps had idealized Ted Garrett. As in one of Sir Walter Scott's romantic novels, Ted had rescued her from peril. And their one meeting, their tryst, as she amusedly referred to it in her mind, occurred on a romantic evening in a romantic place.

But she did know that he was a gentleman, that he held up the chivalrous ideas that characterized the men of the South. He had treated her with respect and courtesy, actions she certainly did not associate with ruthless Steve Kaptain.

When the dress was ready, Victoria began preparing

herself for the party. She brushed out her hair so that it fell in ebony cascades about her shoulders, and wrapped a yellow knitted shawl about herself, discreetly covering the gown's decolletage. In her never ending attempts at matchmaking, Judith had urged Victoria to wear the shawl, in hopes of attracting one of the single males that made up the larger portion of the wagon train's population.

Judith's efforts, however, were unnecessary, since Victoria's striking comeliness was apparent to all. She had only to pick up a pail, and half a dozen young men were there to help her. All of which Steve found vastly amusing. His amusement at her expense irritated her.

"You could learn some manners yourself, Steve Kaptain," she snapped back once. But he had only laughed, his green eyes dancing with mocking lights.

Since Victoria had spent the late afternoon within the wagon she had not seen Ted and the two men accompanying him arrive. Almost shyly, she climbed down from the wagon and approached the blocked-off center of the camp where most everyone had already gathered, clapping their hands and patting their feet in time to the high-spirited music which had just started up.

She looked around at the familiar faces, hesitating beneath a lantern as she saw Ted, standing among some of the other men and looking splendid in his blue military uniform. As if he felt someone watching him, his gray eyes swung round to meet hers, and a brilliant smile broke out in the goldenly handsome face. A river of pleasure rushed through Victoria as Ted left the group and came to her side.

"You're even more beautiful than I remembered,"

he said warmly, taking her hands in his. His eyes roamed over her face hungrily.

"Apparently not beautiful enough to hold you at my side," she replied, trying to keep her tone even and light.

"That is a moment I deeply regretted, Victoria, and am here to make amends for. Will you do me the honor of this dance?"

Smiling up at him, she laid her hand on the arm he proffered and let him lead her out into the center where a few of the braver couples were already dancing. It was a folk tune many of them were familiar with.

Oh say, were you ever in the Rio Grande?
Way, you Rio.
It's there the river runs down golden sand.
For we're bound to the Rio Grande.

And away, you Rio!
Way, you Rio!
Sing fare you well,
My pretty young girls,
For we're bound to the Rio Grande!

Oblivious to the envious looks of the young men about them, Ted and Victoria had eyes for only each other. He moved well to the tempo, holding her at just the proper distance. But his gray eyes did not abide by propriety, mirroring the passion that burned within him like a candle flame. Gentle now, but if fanned by Victoria's own matching ardor, sure to blaze brightly.

The two of them paused only long enough to eat,

loading their tin plates with steaming, juicy meats and hot, buttered cornbread, over which was spooned thick, soupy beans.

It seemed to Victoria that she laughed and enjoyed herself more that night than ever before. She felt young—a feeling that, in spite of her youthful age, she had never experienced. Her anxieties, under the pampered attention Ted showered on her—along with the other young men that were occasionally courageous enough to break in on the lieutenant for a dance—suddenly lifted from her shoulders.

Only the sight of Steve, leaning against an elm, a cigarette held lightly between his lips, dampened her pleasure. Her breath caught with the fear that he would do something to destroy her newly found happiness. It would take only one word from him—and everyone would know that she had worked in a brothel . . . that she had been involved in a murder. Victoria did not think she could have stood to see the light of admiration slowly fade from Ted's wondrously bright eyes.

But when Steve tossed away his cigarette and came forward, it was not to expose her, but to claim Maya for a dance. Roberto, whom Maya had been dancing with, was by this time drunk. He sat with two or three of the older men by one of the back wagons, drinking and sometimes shouting belligerently, so he did not notice as Maya wantonly pressed her voluptuous body against Steve's. But Victoria did. She released her held breath.

Ted whispered something in her ear, and she drew her attention away from the other two just as Maya raised full, red lips to those of Steve's.

"I'm sorry. What did you say, Ted?"

"I said, lovely lady, did you notice the way the stars fall out of the sky tonight? They're like cascades of diamonds."

Victoria turned her face upwards in time to see another shooting star streak across the sky. She breathed a sigh of ecstasy.

Her parted lips told of the delights that waited there for some man to claim, and Ted pulled her closer to him, finding it hard to control the desire this woman stirred in his loins.

The nameless faces spun around them as they whirled about the enclosure of the benches. And yet, Victoria thought, she should have known her happiness was not to last forever. She should have known that Steve would not spare her. That he was not the gentleman Ted was.

As the waltz ended, and Ted released her, Steve said from behind them, "I'd like to claim your partner, Garrett."

The two men faced each other. A small frown creased the bridge of Ted's nose, and he looked to Victoria for her consent. Steve's eyes were noncommittal, but Victoria knew that meant little. He controlled his features so well that she doubted anyone ever really knew what he was thinking.

Not wishing to risk angering Steve, she nodded to Ted. Reluctantly he dropped her hand as Steve pulled her against him so that they were one. From somewhere, it seemed so far away to her with those unyielding dark eyes on her face, the music began again.

Steve's movements were lithe and graceful, but there was a hardness in his body. Victoria wondered if he ever actually relaxed that inner guard or if the years of hardship on the frontier and in captivity had turned his heart and mind to nerveless organs of steel.

His low words broke into her reverie. "I believe, *corazón*, you promised me I'd never see your hair hanging loose about your shoulders."

Victoria looked up into the mocking eyes. "You can be sure, Steve Kaptain, that it wasn't for you I arranged my hair."

His lips narrowed in a long line, and he jerked her against him even more tightly. "You're as big a tease, Vicky, as Maya. And I don't know what makes me want you . . . because you damned sure aren't worth it!"

His admission that he wanted her hit like a bolt of lightning, but she managed to control her surprise. "Then why won't you let me go?" she taunted.

His eyes were as cold and deadly as gun metal. "Because I intend to collect for the trouble you've caused me. And then, for all I care, you can sleep with every saddle bum between here and Santa Fe."

His grip was like a band of iron about her waist, and a soft moan escaped her lips.

"But you damn well better behave yourself until then."

"Or what?" she asked, the audaciousness in her voice hiding her inner trembling.

"Do you need to ask?"

Victoria stared up into those uncompromising eyes and wordlessly shook her head.

XIV

❧❧❧❧❧❧❧❧❧❧❧❧

When Rip Ford and Robert Neighbors rode out of camp the next morning, everyone in the wagon train felt somewhat bereft, as if losing a close neighbor. But Victoria felt it greater than many, for she sensed she was losing a true friend.

"We'll meet again," Rip had promised her, giving her a farewell kiss on the forehead. "Texas isn't that big."

Not long after their departure Steve set the wagon train on the next stage of its trek. Jake rode back to his place behind the train, warning each wagon grimly, "Pull in your belts a notch 'cause the worst is sitting out yonder."

As the day wore on the pioneers themselves came to acknowledge the fact, for the terrain rapidly changed from gently rolling hills to flat, arid plains broken only by groves of twisted mesquite and sweltering brush. The climate changed, too: A dry, slowly-simmering heat rose from the hard-baked earth to meet overhead with the brassy, white-hot sky.

Often Ted would ride back, letting his horse pace itself alongside Victoria's wagon. "The next camp is Horsehead Crossing." His eyes mirrored his concern. "It isn't too much for you, is it?"

"Of course not," she answered, gently flicking the whip as Steve had taught her. "I can do anything any of the other women can."

"Perhaps," he said, "but you're much smaller, more delicate. And much more beautiful," he added with a twinkle in his eye.

She laughed. "You just don't know me." Then, sobering, she asked, "Ted, do you think this Tall Tree can be trusted?"

He tightened his lips and shrugged. "I don't know, Victoria. Both he and Buffalo Hump came highly recommended by way of Legs Lewis, a captain with the Texas Rangers. And, as I understand, General Woolf himself gave the orders to hire the two Penatoka guides."

"Does—does Steve trust him?"

Ted's preoccupied gaze shifted to meet hers. After a moment he said, "You know Steve Kaptain never lets anyone know what he's thinking. But you asked me, and the best I can tell you is no—I don't think Steve trusts Tall Trees. But Steve'll go along with Woolf's command—as long as it suits Steve."

Ironically, it was that same day that Steve, his expression cold and deadly, dismissed Tall Trees—going against the direct orders of General Woolf.

The wagon train had encamped on the Pecos River at Horsehead Crossing, which Jake said got its name from the large number of skeletons of horses' heads. The guide, Tall Trees, had built a campfire off to himself and, due to his laziness, had not banked it properly. A light wind came up and the fire got out of control. The licking flames ate their way toward the wagon camp. The people grabbed their blankets and began beating at the flames.

In the pandemonium the two-year-old Jason got too close, and his clothing caught fire. Screaming, Elizabeth dropped her blanket and ran toward him. Her frantic efforts to strip the clothing from him were of little help. Within seconds Steve was there, wrapping the child in the blanket the woman had dropped and rolling him on the ground.

But by then it was too late. Sobbing hysterically, the woman gathered up the small, lifeless body in her arms. As she sat there in the dust, while the last of the flames were beaten out, she cradled her son and moaned like an animal. Steve tried to help her to her feet.

"Leave me alone!" she screamed. "Don't touch me! "It's all your fault! You're the one that hired that beast. You're responsible for Jason's death!"

Steve's face turned as hard as granite, and his eyes looked down at the woman bleakly. Breaking through the crowd that had gathered, Victoria came to Steve's side. "Mrs. Caldwell," she said gently, taking the child from her, "let's go back to your wagon."

The smell of burnt flesh nauseated Victoria so much her stomach knotted in spasms, but she did not notice the pain because she was crying.

Because of the burial the next morning, it was too late to start out for the Davis Mountains, or the Pahcut Mountains as the Indians called the range, which was forty-eight miles and a full day's march away, and the train was forced to lay over another day.

Gathering at the banks of the Pecos, the pioneers listened with saddened hearts while Ted, acting with the authority of the U.S. government, spoke over the grave, which lay in the midst of the scattered horse skeletons. Victoria thought his brief words simple but well chosen.

Steve stood with his hat in his hands, his green eyes unfathomable. When he looked like that, Victoria had learned to fear him, dreading the harsh words that could lash out like tiny whips. But his lips were stretched tight in impenetrable silence.

After it was all over, Amy led Elizabeth away, and, embarrassed, the others scattered to their various duties. Victoria remained. Viola came up behind her as she stood gazing at the stark and dismal sight.

"There's some things that just ain't right," Viola said, holding her stomach as if protecting the unborn baby. "And I have to sometimes wonder if the Good Lord knows what He's about."

Unable to talk calmly about Jason's death as did Viola, who by that time had become inured to it, Victoria bit her lip, remaining silent.

Sensing this, Viola changed the subject. "You ever wonder, honey, 'bout why all the horseheads?"

Victoria shook her head.

"Jake was telling Jess and me 'bout it. T'was the Mexicans and Comancheros that did it. They drive the Mustangs up here from the border—hell bent for leather. Jake says there's no water 'tween the Rio Grande and here—so them poor critters run right to the Pecos and drink themselves to death, 'stead of slow-like. Then their stomachs cramp up on 'em, and they die. The Comancheros and Mexicans, they just leave those that can't make it here to die."

Victoria looked up at that moment to see Steve striding toward them, and all her bitterness welled up. "I'd be surprised if Mr. Kaptain doesn't do the same to us—leave us here and take his precious rifles on."

She knew she was being unfair, that, acting under orders, Steve had hired the guide. But her hurt was so great, she felt she had to lash out at someone or she would collapse in hysteria like Elizabeth.

"Don't know what's 'tween you two, honey, but you're sure wasting a lot of time."

"Viola, Victoria," Steve said imperiously, "get back to your wagons and get them in a circle," he pointed to a bluff that ran off to their left, "there—out of the wind. Then stay put."

Victoria felt she had taken just about all the orders from Steve she could. "Now wait just—"

"Come on," Viola said, taking Victoria's arm. "Now's not the time for a lovers' tiff."

As if realizing he had been short with them, Steve said, "There's a sandstorm riding in." He pointed to the northwest where an angry purple cloud lay low on the horizon.

161

Viola and Victoria hurried to join the others in moving the wagons while the cloud line climbed swiftly, higher and higher, until the sun was overcast. With a howl the winds came, and everything was blotted out in a blur of swirling sand.

The men tried to corral the animals within the circle of the wagons, but occasionally one of the smaller animals would get caught by the wind and be lifted from its feet and rolled over and tumbled like a ball.

The pioneers' ears and eyes and throats smarted with the sting of the sand. There was a sudden shriek of the storm, and then the wind struck with such force that some of the wagons were lifted and tossed even as were the animals. The wind reached its peak just as the sun set on the horizon, then gradually ebbed away, and all was still.

One by one they climbed down from their wagons to survey the damage, just as Noah had done after the flood.

Judith and Billy Lee's wagon had suffered a broken axle, and the canvas cover had been stripped from it so that it looked like a reefed ship. Many of the other wagons had suffered the same fate.

Her curly red hair coated with sand, Judith knelt in the wagon crying softly with fright and shock. Billy was hopelessly trying to comfort her.

But the Towerses fared the worst in the wagon train. Victoria, worried about the aged couple, was on her way to their wagon when Jess leaned out and called for Steve. "It's old man Towers," he yelled. "Some sort of attack."

Both Steve and Ted left the frightened animals, which had been close to stampeding, and hurried over to the Towers wagon, reaching it just before Victoria did.

Sim lay prostrate in the wagon. "It's his lungs," Amy said, turning up tear-filled eyes to the group about the wagon. "That's why we chose to come west. Instead of starting over in the town where we were."

"Clear out, everyone," Steve ordered. "Get the camp back in shape."

Even as the circle of onlookers began to drift away, Sim Towers's labored breathing came to a halt with a final wheeze. Amy broke down in gasping sobs.

Steve untied the handkerchief from about his neck and wiped away the tears and sand that matted in the wrinkles of Amy's face. He took her frail, shaking hands and said, "Mrs. Towers, your husband was a dignified gentleman. He wouldn't want this from you."

"I'll take over," Victoria told Steve as Amy tried to compose herself. He nodded and went to help Ted, who had put the men to work setting the wagons right and collecting the articles that were scattered about in the sand.

Burdened by the deaths and disasters, the pioneers that evening tried to shake their grief from them with lively song and music. Someone produced a harmonica, and Maya stepped into the intimate circle of fire-light. Slowly she moved about the spectators, sinuously moving her hips and snapping her fingers in time to the tempo. Her movements increased with the music, and her skirts whirled wildly about her well-formed thighs. The slanted golden eyes flirted passionately with Steve, who remained in the flickering shadows of the orange campfire. He watched her through half-closed eyes as her hips thrust and withdrew in invitation.

She was a wild, passionate woman who knew how to make a man happy, when to keep her mouth shut and welcome her lover with open, ever-ready arms. And Steve wondered harshly why Victoria, the small wraith of a woman, should continue to interest him. For since that moment in Reynosa when he had perceived her standing over him, even then intent on murdering him, she had been nothing but a thorn in his side.

As Maya's dance ended among enthusiastic applause and she came willingly to his side, he tossed away his cigarette as he would gladly have liked to Victoria.

Victoria had retired to her wagon early and was brushing out her hair when the sound of the gay music reached her. Her loneliness welled up within her so that she could stand it no longer. Slipping out of her wagon, she sat with her back against one wheel where she could listen to the music and watch the dancing under the cover of darkness.

And as the music ended and she saw Maya slip through the crowd to join Steve, the two moving away together in the darkness, she looked up to see Ted standing quietly by her. His gaze had followed hers, and he looked back at her as the couple disappeared and asked, "It may be none of my business, Victoria, but—no, that's wrong," he said, squatting on one knee so that their faces were only inches apart. "It is my business. Because whatever affects you affects me."

The gray eyes were steadfast as he took her small hands between his larger ones. "Victoria, I'll soon have enough money from some other investments to leave the Army. I want to take you back with me to Virginia. In the style that you deserve. I want you to be my wife—to share my life, Victoria."

He gathered her up against him, and Victoria, feeling the passion that throbbed within him, quivered in response. He rained kisses on her soft hair that waved about her face with a will of its own, on her closed lids with their long, feathery lashes, and her trembling lips.

He put her away from him. "I don't want to rush you, darling. But I've known from that moment I first saw you at Three Rivers. With your eyes sparkling like blue diamonds against the velvety blackness of your hair. When I saw you facing Walker like a haughty princess affronted by her subject, I knew I had to have you for my own."

"And yet, we might never have met again," she whispered, "except for luck."

"It wasn't luck." He smiled down at her. "I'm a determined man."

"What do you mean?"

"I knew you were in San Antonio and I applied for spring leave to find you, when a copy of Steve's report to General Woolf came through my hands."

"Steve's report?"

"Yes," Ted answered, his face puzzled. "Steve volunteered to lead this train through to El Paso. Everyone that went on this trip had to be cleared through headquarters. Your name was listed as—as . . ."

"As what, Ted?"

His gray eyes met hers with a direct look. "As a cook."

Victoria's face mirrored her confusion, and Ted went on. "During the Mexican-American war the soldiers that volunteered for dangerous duty were sometimes known to list as cooks the women they took along as their—well, camp followers."

"Camp followers!" she repeated, her eyes blazing like blue-hot coals in the whiteness of her face.

Ted nodded. "The military winks an eye at the practice in order to encourage more volunteers."

"And you—you thought that I was a—a camp follower?"

"No," Ted said, pulling her against him. "But I did know, at least, that you would be going to El Paso. That's why I jumped at the chance to replace Ford and Neighbors when they were reassigned to Rio Grande City.

"Victoria, if you have any problems, I want to help you. But I need to know if Steve means something to you. If he does, I'll leave you alone."

"He is nothing to me!"

"Then give me your answer, darling. Don't make me wait."

Victoria looked down at her hands, trying to gather her thoughts, but her fury was so great that there was only room in her heart at that minute for the hate she felt for Steve. He was contemptible! Despicable! There was nothing he would not do, she told herself, to achieve his ends. Listing her as a camp follower! A common slut! All so that he could bed her again.

She would show him. She would indeed marry Ted. She would put herself beyond Steve Kaptain's rapacious hands!

She raised Ted's palm to her face and rubbed it against her cheek. "If the offer still stands, Ted, I'll marry you at the very next settlement that has a minister."

XV

✻✻✻✻✻✻✻✻✻✻✻✻

Now that the days would be growing hotter, the pioneers were forced to rise even earlier in order to get on their way before the boiling sun rose on the horizon.

The morning following the sandstorm, Victoria rose while the sky was still dark and the semidesert air still frigid. She desperately wanted a bath, feeling she could no longer endure the sweaty odor that clung to her clothes and permeated her skin. Yet a bath that morning was unthinkable, not only because of the extreme cold, but also because there were no large trees or high banks to conceal her from view of the wagons. She knew she would have to be content with bathing her face and neck, and for once she envied the near-naked Indians who did not have to put up with long sleeves and cloying petticoats that grew sticky with sweat as the day wore on.

She had thought she was the only one awake, but as she knelt at the bank, she perceived instantly that there was someone there near her. As if coming silently on cat feet, Steve was there. His Indianlike movements still unnerved her, and she jumped to her feet.

She heard his low chuckle and saw the metallic flash of his gun in the darkness as he released the cocked hammer, shoving the gun into the holster strapped at his thigh. "If you're going to wander from camp like that, you ought to give a warning. I almost shot you."

"I wasn't planning on meeting anyone," she said shortly. "And, besides, I might ask the same of—"

"Shhhh," he said, covering her mouth with his hand. "It seems I am about to be proved right."

Victoria did not understand what he was talking about, nor did she hear anything, but was only conscious of being held tightly against him from behind. Then, as the pink light of day suddenly splashed over the tableland, Victoria saw Ted leading his horse by the bridle.

Steve released her, and she was about to call out to Ted when, before she could understand what happened, Steve's hand went to his hip in one rapid movement, and the orange burst of fire exploded from his gun.

At the same moment Ted's horse shied. Ted released the bridle and doubled over. As Victoria and Steve ran toward him, he tore at his pants leg just above his boot. He looked up at them, a growing horror suffusing his face.

At his feet lay curled a rather small snake with rattlers. Its head was shattered. "A sidewinder," Steve said grimly, catching Ted as he seemed to sag.

"I—I didn't see it," Ted said, stunned.

"Quick, Vicky," Steve said. "Try and hold him up."

With no wasted movements, Steve unbuckled his belt and strapped it around Ted's thigh, above the wound. Already, where the skin was exposed, red streaks climbed upward. As Steve prepared to cut the slightly puffed skin around the puncture wound, Victoria recognized the knife as the one he had lent her to slice the bacon. So long ago, she thought, and yet it was only a little less than a month.

Ted moaned as Steve deftly wielded the knife, and Victoria turned her head when Steve put his dark head to the leg and began to suck and spit, suck and spit.

"Okay, Vicky," he said at last. "Can you help me get him back to the wagon?"

Ted's face was chalky white. "Is he going to be all right?"

"If I got all the poison out—if we can keep the fever down—if he doesn't get an infection."

Between the two of them, they supported Ted, starting back to the wagon where some of the people had gathered to watch, a few of them only half dressed.

Viola came down to meet them. "I already got hot water boiling, Steve."

"Good!"

Steve's green eyes fixed on Victoria. "Can Ted share your wagon? He's going to need a lot of attention the next few days. And yours isn't as crowded as the others."

Victoria thought of the rifles, but she knew what Steve said was true. She had not brought the keepsakes, the clothing, the small bits of furniture most of the others had. There were no children, no husbands to share her wagon.

She nodded in agreement, and they moved off toward her wagon with Ted still between them, his boots dragging in the dust. Supported on one side by Steve's height and on the other by Victoria's diminutiveness, Ted's body hung at an extreme angle.

When they reached the wagon, Victoria climbed in and began making room. Steve swung Ted up into his arms like Ted was a baby, lifting him into the rear of the wagon. While they waited for Viola to bring the hot water, Victoria tried to make Ted comfortable, loosening his shirt and propping his head on a flour sack. She looked up to find Steve watching her intently. The moment passed, and he turned away, his bronzed face expressionless.

Shortly after the wound had been cleaned and bandaged, the wagon train got under way, looking from above like a wounded snake as it crawled across the expanse of desert. Since Victoria also had to drive the wagon, caring for Ted became a strenuous task. Every so often she would be forced to halt the wagon as perspiration oozed from him and wordless sounds poured from his pale lips. So as not to hold up the others, Steve assigned her wagon to the rear, where Jake could lend a hand when necessary.

The day seemed interminable to Victoria. Nothing higher than sagebrush grew to break the horizon, and

170

there was no shade from the boiling sun. The dust kicked up from the wagons ahead of Victoria's hovered motionlessly in the air before falling back to the scorching ground. As the Pah-cut Mountains rose on the distant horizon, the terrain became rougher, more rocky, with precipitous ridges.

In spite of the constant care Victoria gave Ted, he seemed to grow worse. That evening they camped on the banks of the Tojah River, forty feet wide and swift. Victoria did not leave the wagon but tried to spoon-feed Ted some chicken broth Viola had made. But he tossed and moaned, so that more broth spilled on him than ran into his mouth.

Sometime during the night, while Ted moved restlessly, Steve came. Stifling a small cry of surprise, Victoria said, "Steve, I'm worried. He's not doing any better."

She could barely see his face in the darkness of the night, but somehow it was reassuring to know he was there. "Ted's going through the crisis now, Vicky. Tomorrow'll tell us. Look, there's not a breath of air in here. My saddle and blanket's out there where it's cooler. Go stretch out and get yourself some rest. I'll watch Ted."

She looked doubtful, and he said, "I'll wake you at daybreak. I promise."

Worried as she was, she fell asleep immediately, comforted by the smells that enveloped her. Steve, she remembered, had told her everyone had his own particular smell. The odor of tobacco, leather, and something like newly scythed hay that mingled with perspiration belonged to Steve, she decided with her last waking thoughts.

171

It seemed to her that only a few minutes had passed when a hand was on her shoulder, gently shaking her awake. She opened sleepy eyes, dimly perceiving Steve's outline.

"Steve, how is he?"

"The fever's broke. But he's still very weak. Daybreak's in a few minutes. Why don't you wash up? You'll feel better."

With something akin to gratefulness for Steve, she slipped down to the banks of the Tojah. Here and there were a few scraggly cottonwood trees. She stepped out of her foul-smelling skirts and blouse, not caring whether Steve's sharp eyes saw her or not, and waded until the cold water rose to her knees. Almost with sensuous pleasure she splashed clean her dirt-encrusted body, feeling revived and fresh.

She dreaded donning her filthy clothes but, much to her dismay, there was no need to. At the place where she had left her clothes heaped in a mound was the soft leather Indian dress she had stored away so angrily. She knew Steve had to have placed it there. But when?

A blush spread over her as she saw Steve replenishing the campfire. The smell of parched coffee drifted to her, and she hesitantly made her way to Steve's side. About them others were crawling out of and from beneath their wagons, stretching and yawning in the early morning light.

"Your clothes are downstream drying on a scrub brush," Steve said, and handed her a cup of coffee.

Silently she accepted the cup, carefully sipping the steaming black liquid. She was uncomfortably aware of Steve's unconcealed amusement. "Thank you."

"Your thanks are not what I want, *corazón*."

She looked up from her cup swiftly to encounter Steve's green-flecked eyes. Her own flashed back. "That's all you're going to get!"

"And that's more like your old, spirited self. I was beginning to worry. Thought maybe you were coming down sick."

Victoria stomped off to her wagon, sloshing hot coffee on her hands. Ted was awake, and his wide gray eyes brightened when he saw her. "Victoria," he said weakly.

Gently she brushed the perspiration-damp locks from the pale face. "How do you feel?"

"Like an old man." Dark circles rimmed the steady eyes that looked at her so lovingly. His lips were dry and cracked, and she lifted his head so that the cup met his lips. As he swallowed the coffee, his throat worked painfully.

His eyes sought hers. "You haven't changed your mind since the night before last, have you?"

She smiled tenderly. "I'm more determined than ever to be your bride."

The joy that lit his eyes banished the guilt she felt, for she found it hard to separate and distinguish her emotions. Life on a wagon train was lived at a more intense level; the basic drive for survival both colored and distorted everything else out of proportion. Perhaps she did love him, but she silently vowed that, either way, she would do everything in her power to make him happy, to be a good wife to him.

"When I'm better, I plan to make you the most envied woman in Virginia. There's so much I want to

173

give you. Just to see your smile, Victoria, is a reward in itself."

Seeing the conversation was tiring him, she said, "Hush, darling," and kissed his brow. "You need to rest. The sooner you're better, the sooner I can become Mrs. Garrett." Reluctantly he released her hand, and she slipped out of the wagon.

She went about her work that morning with a singing heart, the joy growing in it with each lingering thought of Ted's warm love. She told herself that fortune had not turned its face from her after all. That perhaps the Lord, in His wisdom, had allowed all that happened to her previously to prepare her for this. To bring her to the wilderness to meet Ted Garrett once again.

By the time the wagons rolled out, she had grown to accept the idea of being his wife, and, like a bride, she shyly climbed into the wagon seat, blushing with the knowledge that her betrothed was only inches away. She turned slightly to glimpse the handsome, sensitive face.

He slept deeply, his breathing light, but his face was damp with perspiration. She worried how far the train would have to travel that day, if Ted could sustain the rigorous travel. She called out behind her to Jake, asking him how far to the next encampment.

He rode alongside them, and beneath the brim of his feathered hat his gaze went past her to the inside of the wagon. The mouth in his beard-stubbled jaw was solemn. "It's only eighteen miles southwest of here. At the base of the Pah-cuts. But between here and Mescalero Springs is a lot of rough going."

Several times during that day she was forced to

pause longer than usual; to give Ted water, to bathe his face, or change the bandage. Once, when she was putting away the canteen, she turned to see Steve ride up, his face set in harsh lines.

"Get the team going, Vicky. If you fall any further behind, the wagon train'll have to leave you."

"What about Jake? Can't he stay with us until we catch up?"

"No chance. I'm having to send Jake out to scout. We've got tracks of Indian ponies about. Now get!" Ruthlessly Steve brought his hand down hard on one horse's rump, and the startled animals plunged ahead.

The wagon bounced over the rutted earth and Victoria heard Ted moan. Her thoughts turned viciously to Steve. There was nothing gentle about the man. She detested his strength, his indifference, his hardness.

Still, she promised herself, Steve would be defeated for once. A brittle smile came to her lips as she swore she would outwit him at his game.

When the sun had passed its zenith in the copper sky and was on its descent, the wagons reached Mescalero Springs and formed their horseshoe near a cluster of cherry trees. Victoria was exhausted and her back ached. But she was worried by the dull redness that flushed Ted's face. She helped him to sit up, but his hands were indeed as feeble as an old man's as he tried to drink the water she offered him.

When a little later Viola appeared with a plate of mashed beans, she said, "Why, honey, you're glowing like a lamp. I declare you're plumb beautiful today." Her thin-lashed eyes searched Victoria's face shrewdly. "You ain't in love with that soldier man, are you?"

Shyly, Victoria wiped her grimy hands on her skirt

before smiling into Viola's toil-worn face. "Ted's asked me to be his wife, Viola. I—I wanted you to be the first to know."

Viola nodded and said, "Getting yourself a good man. But good men don't necessarily guarantee happy unions."

Preoccupied with Viola's enigmatic words, Victoria at first did not notice Ted's own silence as she attempted to get him to eat the beans. But when he smiled at her, his eyes were shadowed, and she soon realized something was troubling him.

"Darling, what is it? Can I get you some more water?"

He shook his head wordlessly and crossed one arm over his forehead. "Just stir-crazy," he mumbled against the thickness of the dark blue shirt.

Of course, she thought. She should have known. Ted was a man of action and, like all men hampered by illness, he fretted at his enforced idleness.

"You'll feel better after the sun has set. It'll be cooler. Perhaps we can arrange for a bath."

Ted removed his arm and gave her a mocking grin. "What? And have you see me naked before our wedding?"

Victoria knew she should have been shocked, but she could not help but laugh. It was such a relief to see some of Ted's former liveliness return.

Realizing that Ted wasn't well enough to bathe in the springs, Victoria had Jake bring a small tub of water she had heated to the wagon where she proceeded to sponge-bathe Ted. Teasing him, he allowed her to remove his shirt. And as she cleansed away the sweat and dust, he told her about Virginia, the beauty of its land, the history of its people—so vividly described that she could almost share his pride.

When she peeled away the sticky bandage around Ted's leg, he ceased talking, and she knew without looking at the swollen red flesh that he was in pain. Carefully she rebandaged the wound, emptying the bloody water out of the back of the wagon. She was glad Ted was too worn out with the evening's exertion to notice her own silence.

The leg was worse. She knew she would have to talk to Steve. He would have to be told of Ted's condition.

Yet how she loathed having to depend on the very man she so detested. She blew out the lantern, and, as she had done once before, went in search of Steve Kaptain.

XVI

✼✼✼✼✼✼✼✼✼✼✼

Maya, Roberto, Jess, and several others sat at one of the nearby campfires, their laughter giving the camp a civilized atmosphere there in the midst of the wilderness. Victoria hesitated asking them where Steve was, not wanting to see the smirk on Maya's face. Looking about, she spotted Judith outside her wagon cleaning up the supper dishes.

"Judith," she called, crossing to the wagon, "do you know where Steve Kaptain is?"

Judith brushed a strand of hair from her face with the back of her hand and smiled impishly. "I knew it,

Victoria. I knew you'd find yourself a man. And a lieutenant in the Army at that. It's absolutely romantic!"

So people already knew. Victoria wondered anxiously if Steve had heard yet. "Yes, it's true, Judith. But Ted needs medical attention. He needs a doctor. I have to find Steve. Have you seen him?"

Judith's freckled skin creased in a frown as she tried to remember. "It's been some time. He and Jake were talking, heading toward those old ruins."

Victoria knew of the ruins, the leftover rubble of a Spanish post, that were just beyond the cherry grove and the tethered horses. Thanking Judith, she hurried on, passing the Towers wagon. From within came the sounds of soft crying. She paused uncertainly, not knowing if she should try to comfort the old woman. Yet, she felt that Amy would feel better if she could cry the grief out of her heart.

And, forcing herself to be honest, she had to admit that there was the greater urge to find Steve, to also seek relief from worry in relating to him Ted's worsened condition.

The arching branches of the cherry trees blotted out the satin moon riding high in the black velvet sky, and Victoria groped her way past the trees and staked-out horses into the open again. There the moonlight displayed for her the decaying ruins, the remains of a civilization that had ceased to exist. She peered out among the scattered stones and the grotesquely half-broken walls that had once enclosed rooms. But she saw no human form.

One of the horses whinnied, and from afar she heard the eerie cry of a coyote. She thought of turning back, of seeking the familiar security of the wagon-encircled campfires.

Still determined to find him, she wandered beyond the ruins, watching her footing as she rounded a low bluff. "Steve," she called out softly above the clatter of the rolling pebbles her foot had scattered.

A hand clamped itself over her mouth. She struggled frantically against the iron-tight arm that encircled her waist, lifting her from the ground so that her legs kicked furiously in the air.

"Will you shut up," Steve hissed.

She bit his hand, and he jerked her head back against his shoulder. Her body arched with the pain, but he did not relinquish her until she ceased flailing the empty air. When he unexpectedly loosed his hold, she slumped weakly against him, and he caught her once more even as he pushed her down against the ground alongside him. One leg he threw across her.

"I've never known one woman to make so much noise," he whispered.

She jerked away from the hands that held her, wondering what it was about his touch that disturbed her so, searing her skin like a poker iron—as if he were putting his own brand on her.

"That coyote was making more noise than I was, Steve Kaptain!"

"That was no coyote, my dear."

"What—what was it?"

Steve's rugged face was only inches from her own, his eyes burning in the darkness like tiny green fires. "It appears we may have visitors."

"Indians?"

"Mescaleros."

181

"When?"

"Don't know. Might be days from now. Might be at dawn. Jake's gone to find out."

"Oh, Steve, what are we going to do? Ted needs help—now!"

She felt rather than saw the frown. "He's worse, then?"

"Yes. He needs a doctor. How far is it to the closest settlement?"

A slow smile spread across his angular face. "Is it a doctor—or a man of God that makes you so anxious?"

"I—I don't know what you're talking about?"

"Come off it, Vicky. I know you too well."

"All right, then. Yes. Ted has asked me to marry him. And there's nothing you can do about it, Steve! Do you hear me? Not one damned thing!"

"I could refuse to get a doctor for him. After all, the interest of the entire wagon train comes first."

Her breath whistled in a ragged gasp between gritted teeth. "You wouldn't dare!"

"No, I wouldn't. What you don't understand, *corazón,* is that not even a ring will keep you from me if—and when—I want you." His voice had a lazy drawl, made the more chilling by its very lack of emotion.

Victoria stiffened, by now recognizing the danger that lay hidden beneath its deceptive softness. Slowly his arms tightened about her, until he held her crushed against his own hard body.

"I would suggest that you make the payment you owe me before you and Ted come together in holy matrimony." His warm, tobacco-scented breath fanned her cheeks. "Because afterwards, your payment could definitely be considered grounds for adultery."

"You would have to rape me first," she said icily. "And that would definitely be considered grounds for hanging."

"On the contrary, *corazón*. I won't have to rape you. You'll come to me quite willingly."

"I'll burn in hell first!"

"And would you hurt Ted with the knowledge of your tarnished past? That pedestal he has you on would crumble quicker than the walls of Jericho."

"You wouldn't tell him!"

His slow smile gleamed wickedly in the darkness. "Do you dare to test me?"

Her eyes searched the dark face for a sign of leniency, but there was none there. "Shall I raise my skirts and spread my legs like the whore you believe me to be?" she asked contemptuously.

She rolled from him and began tugging at her skirts, but Steve caught her wrists. For a moment he said nothing, and she wondered if it was the same contempt she felt for him that she saw mirrored in his own eyes. He released her, shoving her from him. "I happen to be a man who prefers to choose his own time."

"You're wrong there, Steve."

One dark brow arched questioningly.

"You're not a man. You're an animal." She was amazed at the coolness she felt, for surely, she thought, he would kill her then.

Nothing happened, and she realized he was silently laughing. "Get back to camp," he said at last, "before I treat you like the whore you're acting."

When she arrived back at the wagon, Ted was tossing and moaning, his fever on the rise again. She tried to bathe his forehead, and he shoved her hand away. "My horse. Where is he? Where's Rider?"

Victoria almost laughed that it was the horse Ted was so concerned about and not the possibility of an infection. "Rider's tied to the back of our wagon, darling. Now stop worrying."

But when Ted said emphatically, "Don't let anyone near Rider!" she knew he was delirious and indeed worse.

Much later she tried to get some sleep, tossing as restlessly in the crowded wagon as did Ted. She knew that Steve had been right. That she had acted like a whore. It seemed all her good intentions to behave in a dignified manner fled like the wild mustangs whenever she was around Steve.

And she acknowledged he was right—that the peril the Mescaleros presented to the wagon train was definitely more important than the danger of gangrene in Ted's leg. She finally fell asleep, just before dawn, tortured by Ted's low groans and Steve's mocking words—and the putrid smell of rotting flesh.

Her fear of an Indian attack was somewhat dissipated when dawn came peacefully, growing into another white-hot day. The men and women gathered desultorily about the campfires. They were hungry, for it was the last of the bacon that sizzled in the skillets that morning, bacon which the children would eat. The game had been scarce, and, since coming into Apache territory, Steve had forbidden the use of firearms. And they were afraid. Their eyes looked bleakly at one another. The word had spread that there were signs of Mescaleros.

All of them turned expectantly as Steve approached. The way he took off his hat and wiped his arm across his forehead told Victoria that the mental strain of the watch had cost him more than just a sleepless night. He carried the burden of all their lives. For that moment Victoria put aside her hatred of Steve.

She made her way through the people that had gathered about him and handed him a cup of hot coffee which she had initially poured for herself. Silently Steve took the cup. The sage-green eyes in the tanned face showed an unconcealed look of surprise at her thoughtful gesture. But then the long lids drooped lazily, concealing whatever thoughts lay beneath.

Slowly he sipped the bitter liquid. Some of the men shuffled impatiently but dared not push him. They knew, as Victoria had come to know, that Steve would tell them in his own good time exactly what they needed to know and no more.

When he finished the coffee, he set his hat on his head, tilting the brim low over his eyes as a shade against the bright morning sun.

"Lieutenant Garrett needs a doctor badly," Steve said, while his penetrating gaze moved over each of them. Only briefly, it seemed to Victoria, did his piercing eyes rest longer on her than the others. "The nearest doctor is at Fort Davis. Fifty miles due south. El Paso still lies a hundred and fifty miles east of us. With the Salt Draw to cross in between. If we get to the draw after the spring floods have filled it, we may have a two or three-week wait. The decision is yours to make."

Roberto Duval edged forward. "Hell, Kaptain, isn't it your job to guide us?" His square, beard-stubbled jaw jutted forward. "Didn't the Army pay you to get us there?"

Steve stuck his thumbs in his belt loops. His eyes were deadly in the unsparing face. "I'll get you there, Duval. The decision is the wagon train's as to when."

"What about the Mescaleros, sir?" young Billy Lee asked.

Steve shrugged. "They've been following us for two days now."

"Why didn't you tell us before this?" It was Roberto again, his face growing more belligerent by the moment.

"Would it have made any difference? There's nothing we can do till they're ready to attack. The Mescaleros'll choose their own battleground. Jake's out scouting signs now."

Victoria shivered, remembering the horrible tales of torture and cruelty she had heard about the Indians. She thought she might be able to die bravely but doubted whether she could endure the savage treatment she had heard the Indians gave their unfortunate captives.

"What about food?" someone demanded.

"I saw a corn field just down stream," Jess volunteered.

"It belongs to the Mescaleros," Steve said. Everyone's face fell. "But whether we take the corn of not'll make little difference to them at this point."

Everyone started talking at once, giving their opinion as to what should be done. Steve watched them, a thin, sardonic smile playing over the inscrutable face. Slowly, the voices ebbed as each realized they did not have the courage to speak aloud their fears, their selfishness.

It was Amy, her face still etched with sorrow, who finally spoke. "It appears to me that since Victoria and Lieutenant Garrett are betrothed, the decision should be left to her."

Several heads nodded in agreement. Steve's gaze lighted on Victoria, faintly amused. He had won, Victoria thought. He had forced the decision on her after all.

Helplessly, she looked around at the faces that confronted her. Stringent Elizabeth, who had watched little Jason burn to death, Billy Lee and Judith, who had lost most of their treasured wedding gifts in the sandstorm, Amy who had given up her beloved Sim—and all the others.

Victoria knew she did not have the right to demand that all those people take the chance of sacrificing everything for one man. And she knew that Ted would not want her to ask that of them either.

"We'll go on," she said, her voice flat with the knowledge that she may be exchanging Ted's life for theirs and wondering if they realized it—or cared.

There was a murmur of relief as the men and women dispersed. A sense of shame pervaded the air. Victoria turned on Steve. "Well that's what you wanted, wasn't it? Let Ted's death hang over your head!"

"No man escapes death, Vicky," Steve said quietly. There was a sadness in his face she had never seen before. It made him seem more human. She turned her head away, afraid of something she did not want to understand.

Instead, she looked in the distance at the Pah-cuts that lay on the desert like sleeping giants. "What can we do about his leg?"

"If it gets worse, the leg'll have to be taken off."

"What if Ted refuses?"

"He doesn't have that choice. As head guide, I have the last say."

Victoria whirled on him, the tears glistening in her eyes. "And just where do we find a doctor to take it off?"

"I'll take it off myself." His eyes held hers. "That is, if you'll trust me."

"Do you ever give me a choice, Steve?" she asked bitterly.

XVII

✼✼✼✼✼✼✼✼✼✼✼

As it turned out, Victoria never had the choice.

The wagon train was only four hours out of the morning camp, having turned the northern end of the Pah-cuts and heading toward the Diablo Mountains, fifty miles away, when Jake, his sweat-bathed hair hanging in lank strands, rode up alongside the wagon train. Accompanying him, astride a burro, was a small man with a brown, weathered face and a clean-shaven head crisscrossed with scars.

Slowly the wagons rolled to a halt and the teamsters left their perches to gather about Steve and Jake. Victoria turned back to Ted, who lay listlessly in the wagon bed. His skin had an unhealthy gray cast to it.

Brushing the damp hair from his face, she said, "The wagons have halted for a rest," not wishing to cause him to worry over the possible bad news Jake may have brought. "I'll have time to change that bandage."

Ted grasped for her hand. "Victoria, I won't let them cut off my leg. I'll die first!"

"Don't talk like that, Ted! I need you. Is that leg more important than me? Would you give me up before you'd give your leg up?"

She meant only to be persuasive, but she could see she had hurt his feelings. "I can't let you marry a one-legged man, don't you see?" he said, his dulled gray eyes pleading. "What kind of future could I offer you? You deserve better than a cripple."

"Don't be silly, Ted. I'm marrying you for the kind of man you are—inside. If you think your case holds water, then you certainly should not be marrying me, either. One day I'll be as gray and withered as Amy. And that's not exactly what you had in mind when you asked me to marry you, is it?"

Ted's pale lips parted in a smile.

"See how foolish you're talking?"

"All right, Victoria. You know—I believe you're going to be a hard female to keep in rein."

Victoria laughed. "You're just realizing that?" Seeing that the effort to talk had brought a sheen to his face, she said, "Now get some rest while the wagon isn't bumping everywhere. I've got to talk to Judith for a moment."

Instead she made her way to the group that encircled Steve and Jake and the little man with them. The two scouts wore their customarily expressionless look, but there was something ominous about the tightness around their lips. Steve squatted and drew in the sand with a stick while the man who had ridden in with Jake talked.

The wizened man looked jumpy as he recounted his story. "Yep, like I said, I was baptizing Sam Tate's little 'un when there was the sudden-like whoop-and-hollering—enough to curl your backbone—and a band of them Mescaleros burst through the cabin door."

The man paused to look nervously about him, and someone said, "Well, get on with it, Caleb. What happened next?"

The man, Caleb, rubbed his bald head. "Well there, I done been close enough to them Indians before. Somewhere one of them red sons of Satan got my hair hanging in his tepee for a trophy. Closest shave I ever had—don't need another one, thank you just the same, Lord. Anyway, I started acting crazy-like—they're superstitious about the insane—and spouting off gibberish, and they left me alone. While they's doing all their butchering to that poor Tate family—God have mercy on their souls—I just walked out the door easy like. I was hightailing it down the Salt Draw on Sally"—he paused to pat the burro's bony flanks—"when I met up with your scout here."

"What's this mean to us, Steve?" Jess asked.

Steve looked up, his eyes glinting like mirrors beneath the brim of his hat. "Better let Jake tell you."

The hard-boiled frontiersman hunkered next to Steve. "Well, folks, it comes down to this. Some ten miles dead ahead is the Salt Draw. Perfect place for fording—wide yet shallow."

He drew a line in the sand representing the draw. "But right before you get there are the Sentinella foothills—filled with plenty of good ambush places. Now six miles further north the draw is deep and swift—and some of you'd most likely lose your teams and wagons if you crossed there. But the area round there is open. No place for the Mescaleros to hide."

"Did you see any signs of them?" someone asked.

Jake shook his head. "Not around the foothills."

He turned to look at Steve. "But I don't feel right about the place. Went back there three times. The foothills appear safe. Just the same, I don't like the looks of 'em."

Steve stood up and brushed the dust from his pants. "Either way, you're taking a chance," he told the group. "Based on what Jake says, I'd advise you to ford ten miles further up the draw."

"That's easy for you to say," Roberto broke in. "You ain't got anything to lose."

Victoria was tempted to speak out, remembering the load of rifles Steve had invested in, but she held her tongue. For there was also Ted to consider. If her wagon was swept away by the draw's swift current, there would be little hope for Ted to survive, in his condition.

It was Maya who defended Steve. "You stupid louts!" she sneered, facing them with clenched fists on her hips. "Steve Kaptain was hired because he knew more than the rest of us about this land. Now are you going to go against his advice?"

As Maya went to stand beside Steve, Roberto's nostrils flared, and his eyes narrowed murderously. "You all heard the scout," he shouted. "There's no signs of

Indians at the Sentinellas. You want to risk all you got to make a new start by crossing at the deep part of the draw?"

"Damn difficult choice," Billy Lee said, putting his arm about Judith. "But without no proof of Indians . . . and the fact we'd save time by crossing at the pass . . . well, begging your pardon, sir," he said, looking at Steve, "I don't know but what the foothills seem the best of two evils."

There was a noise of general agreement, and Jess said, "Don't want to go against you, Steve. But unless you're dead set against the foothills, I think we've pretty well decided we'd rather cross there."

Steve pulled the hat brim lower over his eyes. "Can't out-argue all of you. It's your choice. Get the wagons rolling."

"One moment," Maya said. "Caleb?"

The spry little man turned to look at the voluptuous woman. The expression on his face was guarded, as if he saw the embodiment of man's temptation.

"Are you one of those circuit-riding preachers? The kind that marries?"

"Yes'm. Close to sixteen year I been ministering the Word of God out here to the forsaken."

Maya looked at Victoria with dancing eyes. "Wouldn't you like to ride into El Paso as Mrs. Ted Garrett?"

Victoria did not know what to say. Marrying Ted had seemed like some action in the distant future. She glanced at Steve, but his expression told her nothing. It was one of total disinterest.

Viola stepped forward. "I think that's up to Ted,

isn't it? After all, he ain't exactly feeling like a spring chicken right now."

"If Victoria'll have me," a voice said from behind them, "I'm ready . . . this very minute."

The crowd parted, and a skeletal looking Ted Garrett both weaved and hobbled toward Victoria. His exertion had brought perspiration to his temples and above his dry, cracked lips. He swayed and Billy Lee caught him, pulling Ted's arm over his shoulder.

Victoria hurried to Ted and placed his other arm about her own shoulder. In the clearing the others had made, the three of them were left standing with Jake, Maya, and Steve. From somewhere Caleb produced a small, battered copy of the Bible.

Victoria was only half-conscious of the words Caleb pronounced over them, but it seemed only seconds later Ted squeezed her hand and placed a feather-light kiss on her lips.

There was a sudden cheer from the people gathered about them, and she looked away from Ted to see Maya's pleased expression. There was the satisfied smile of a cat about her full red lips.

"God bless you both," Caleb said.

Viola gave Victoria a bear-like hug and pecked Ted embarrassedly on the cheek. "My best wishes for you young'ns."

Victoria was surprised to see the tears in her eyes and even more surprised at the tears in her own. Her wedding day was a lot different than she could have ever suspected.

One by one the others congratulated them, before climbing into their wagons. All but Steve. He was nowhere to be seen.

XVIII

✚✚✚✚✚✚✚✚✚✚✚

"Are you ready to go, Mrs. Garrett?" There was a bright smile on Ted's face, but his heavy frame seemed to sag against Victoria, and he tried to straighten.

"Yes, darling. But you're not. Now don't argue. Billy Lee, will you help us?"

Ted was too weak to protest as Billy Lee and Victoria helped him back to the wagon. His breathing was labored, and Victoria bit her lip with worry as they laid him as gently as possible in the wagon's bed.

"You'll be all right as soon as we get to the draw. I can get some water and cool you off."

Ted opened his eyes. "Our marriage is starting

off—on the wrong foot," he whispered. "I want a wife . . . not a mother. Now stop your worrying about me, Victoria."

Reluctantly, she left him and took her seat at the front. The horses moved into their place at the end of the wagon train as she popped the whip over their backs. Jake brought up the rear.

Once, when the scout was close enough to call out to without disturbing Ted's restless sleep, Victoria asked him about Ted's leg, if something could be done about it when they made camp that evening. "He's so adamant about keeping his leg, Jake," she concluded, her black-fringed eyes anxious.

"Many a man's lost more than a leg and lived to make himself useful." The sun-baked face softened for a minute, and he added, "But don't fret about it, missy. We'll look at the leg tonight."

The late afternoon sun was hidden on the horizon by large boulders of white stone streaked with red that formed almost perpendicular cliffs. These Sentinella foothills were actually a series of passes that would lead the wagon train out onto the Salt Draw. As they approached the first of these, Steve rode back along the train, stopping at each wagon. When he came to Victoria's wagon, his face was as impassive as ever. "You got a gun, Vicky?"

She shook her head. "Not unless you count the rifles of yours."

"Here, then. Take this one. Do you know how to use it?"

Again she shook her head.

Steve grimaced, but drew out his other Colt. "Just aim the sight at the end of the barrel—here," he said, indicating on his own six-shooter, "and slowly but firmly pull the trigger."

"Do you think they're out there, Steve? The Mescaleros?"

Steve turned in the saddle and looked about him. His lips were pressed together in a thin line. "They're out there, all right. Somewhere. But what they mean to do—" he shrugged.

For that next hour, it seemed like providence had brought the wagon train safely through the Sentinellas. All the wagons had crossed the shallow Salt Draw to the far side, and Victoria deemed it safe enough to halt for water, which would be cool and refreshing for Ted, who was feverish. She planned to catch up with the train in a few moments.

Jake had ridden off several hundred yards to scout signs while she took the opportunity to fill her canteen. When she looked up, Jake was riding hard toward her, his horse flying over the ground like Pegasus.

"Attack!" he shouted. "Attack!"

Behind him, flowing from crevices in the rocks like erupting lava, were what seemed to Victoria hundreds of near-naked Indians on horseback. For a moment Victoria watched in fascination as the Indians drew their arrows and fired them at Jake.

As he galloped toward the wagon train, the arrows falling harmlessly around him, Victoria dropped the canteen and ran for the wagon. From behind came the thunderous sound of pounding hooves, and she screamed as she was swept up over the back of a horse.

With all her strength she kicked and pounded her

fists against her captor. Above the din of the hideous war whoops she heard Jake shout, "It's me, missy."

The Mescaleros rode close enough now for Victoria to see the vermilion streaks across their faces. She noticed that Jake kept to the right of the war party, so that the mounted bowmen were unable to use their bows on them.

Only once did Jake fire his gun—when one of them only a few yards away raised his arm to sling a tomahawk. The explosion of gunfire was deafening. The faceless Indian slipped from his horse.

When Jake and Victoria rode alongside the wagon train, she viewed the kaleidoscope of horror with distant numbness—as if looking at old tintype pictures—the already burning canvases, Jess's frenzied whipping of his team, Amy's expression of helpless dismay as an arrow pierced her shoulder.

Only then did Victoria realize that, still riding to the right of the Mescaleros, Jake was now riding away from the train. "Jake," she yelled. "Ted. He's alone! We've got to go back for him!"

Jake shook his head grimly. "No chance," he yelled back.

"You're not going to try and help them?"

Jake spurred the horse even faster. "Whether we help or not, they're all going to die."

Victoria struggled then to escape his hold. Perhaps she would have succeeded had he not slammed his fist up under her chin. "Sorry, missy," she heard him say as the pale blue sky above her turned black in a painful haze.

A little later she opened her eyes. Overhead a line of smoke penciled the sky, and in the far distance were faint cries and the sharp crack of rifle fire. She knew she could not have been unconscious long, for there were still orange streaks of sunlight on the horizon. She shifted her weight against the uncomfortable pace of the horse.

"Are you all right, missy?" Jake held her impersonally.

She looked up into that weather-beaten face and nodded. She was still angry, yet subconsciously she knew Jake had done the only sensible thing.

Tears stung her eyes when she thought of the fate of the others, and she squeezed her lids tightly closed against the thought of the unspeakable atrocities that would even now be taking place. "Are they all dead, Jake?"

He slowed the horse some. "Yep—or they soon will be . . . if they're lucky. The damned wagons hampered those folks. No chance for them to escape."

"And Steve?"

"If he was foolhardy enough to stay and fight." Jake's mouth tightened. "Then I wouldn't give a plugged nickel for his life."

The hideous thought of Ted lying helpless in the wagon bed churned in her stomach like spoiled food, and she quickly changed the subject. "Where are we going?"

"To Sierra Diablo. That far peak there."

Victoria knew she had heard that name before. "Steve's ranch is somewhere near there, isn't it?"

"Yes'm."

The mention of Steve's name again brought his image vividly to her mind. And she knew that as much as she had hated him, as many times as she had pitted her will against him and lost, there was also that certain something that bound the two of them together. And the severing of it was almost as painful as the severing of a limb. The thought of that brought back Ted, and Victoria closed her eyes, willing drowsiness to come.

The sky was black, with a thousand stars, and fragrant pines spiraled upwards when next she opened her eyes. "Almost there," Jake said, somehow sensing she had awakened.

Victoria ached everywhere from the one-position travel arrangement, and she shivered in the cold mountain air. Yet she did not dare to complain. She knew she was lucky to be alive.

Almost an hour later they came into a clearing. At its center, on a slight rise, stood a cabin built of logs. Beside it was a lean-to. In the darkness it loomed larger than it actually was. Jake dismounted, and she slid into his arms with a small groan.

"Careful, missy. Some tricky footing ahead."

The door gave open easily, and from somewhere Jake produced a tinder box. Soon the kerosene lamp spread a soft glow over the room.

Victoria looked about her. There was a bed with animal skins thrown over it, a pine washstand with an empty row of pegs next to it, a rough cupboard, and an oblong table with benches.

But what surprised her was the shelf of books over the stone fireplace. Beside the hearth was a stack of wood, and Jake began placing some of the logs in the ash-packed fireplace.

Victoria removed a book, Dickens's *A Tale of Two Cities*, from the shelf and wiped a thin coat of dust off her fingers. Glancing at the titles, she realized that Steve Kaptain was an enigmatic man. Had been, she reminded herself.

An undefinable sense of loss welled up, and she put the book back in its place, as if the covers had suddenly burned her. Jake eyed her curiously.

"Hungry, ma'am?"

"A little." She tried to throw off the sense of dejection. "Could I help fix something?"

"We got some jerky." He took a canister from the shelf and removed the lid, shaking its contents. After inspecting it, he said, "Meal's okay. Can you fix corn pone?"

Victoria managed a small smile. "If I don't have someone standing over me."

"It's all yours, missy."

After the sparse supper, Jake propped his back against one side of the hearth and rolled a cigarette. The familiar action reminded her of Steve.

"What was he like, Jake?"

They both knew whom she was talking about. Jake lowered his bushy brows in a furrow. For a moment he didn't say anything. After he lit the cigarette, he frowned. "Tough little *hombre*. I came upon him two or three days out of the Kiowa camp. He was pretty battered, and skinny as a picket fence. I wanted to send him back to relatives, but he wouldn't go. Claimed he didn't have any."

"Steve told me his family had been killed at the same time he was taken captive." Her voice was the only sound in the hushed cabin, but for the hissing of the fire.

"Then he spared you the details."

201

Unaccountably, she wanted to know. "What were they?"

Jake gave a gruff shrug. "About the usual. His father was hacked to death. Butchered. They roped and dragged his mother through prickly pear till she was mangled beyond recognition. And his sister—they raped her. The girl was just six."

Victoria shuddered, and the memory of another girl who had suffered the same flooded her mind. She asked herself if carrying that hate with her had changed anything. Had the Texas Ranger she decided to avenge herself on suffered any under her verbal—and physical—attacks?

She perceived that her persecution of Steve had been worthless, costing her the effort to sustain it, when she could have better directed that energy in another direction.

Sitting in the warmth of the cabin, she made up her mind that she would put her hatred away from her. Put the memories of Steve Kaptain away from her. He was dead now and could no longer disturb her.

Instead, she would make a new beginning. Somehow, somewhere, she would start over. She would yet succeed in Texas.

Later she would think back to this night and realize how foolish she had been to think she could escape the chains of passion that bound Steve and herself.

XIX

✢✢✢✢✢✢✢✢✢✢✢

A hand touched her shoulder. Instantly she was awake.

There was the click of a cocked trigger.

"You're getting old, Jake," the voice mocked. "I could have had your scalp by now."

From near the fireplace Jake slowly released the hammer. Victoria rolled from the bed to a sitting position. The man she thought dead stood before her. In the dying light of the fire his dark face wore a Satanic expression.

"Steve!" she gasped in a whisper.

"Didn't figure on getting you in my bed this soon, *corazón*."

Her old hatred for this one man returned, flashing through her like blinding lightning. She flew at him, her nails ready to rake his cheeks. Steve stumbled under the onslaught, and the saddlebags on his shoulder slipped to the floor with a thud.

She saw then the dark splotch over Steve's shoulder. He crumpled to the floor, his head striking the saddle bags. Jake was there at once, lifting the large man onto the bed. He tried to unbutton the shirt, but a blood-soaked patch of it clung tenaciously to the wound. Victoria cringed as Steve groaned.

"Get the whiskey bottle from my saddlebag," Jake instructed. "It'll loosen the cloth and boil out the wound."

Victoria rummaged through the leather bag until she found the bottle and hurried back to the bed. Jake poured some of the whiskey over the shoulder and began probing the wound, which was matted with cloth and blood.

Steve winced. "Damn it, Jake," he said, his eyes closed against the pain. "I'm not some bull you're going to castrate. Take it easy."

"Arrow get you, son—or bullet?"

"Those bastards didn't have any firearms—yet."

"Yep, think I feel the head."

Steve barely nodded. "Tried to pull the arrow out. Broke off the shaft."

The callused, dirt-grooved fingers continued to probe. Steve's body tensed, then slumped unconscious, as Jake drew forth the arrowhead.

There was the sharp intake of Victoria's breath. "Will he die?"

Jake shot her a piercing look, started to say something, then seemed to change his mind. "Naw. Lost a lot of blood. But no vital organs hurt."

"Can I do something? Anything?"

"Get the coffee going. He'll be coming round soon."

It was midmorning, and Jake was out tending to the horses, when Steve opened his eyes again. Salt pork and beans were cooking over the fire. Steve moaned. "Hell! It's hot."

Putting down Steve's ripped shirt she was mending, Victoria rose from the table. Cautiously, she crossed to the bed. His square jaw was dark with a faint stubble of beard, and his eyes were shadowed with pain and fatigue. But that same sardonic smile hovered about his long lips.

"You don't have to worry. I'm not going to violate you—now. Can you get me some coffee?"

"Can I poison it first?" she asked, but went to get the coffee when he grinned, not waiting for his mocking words.

She was uncomfortably aware that his eyes followed her. She poured the coffee and brought the cup to him. Unsteadily, he sat up, supporting himself on one elbow. He took one sip and handed the cup back to her. "I'm weaker than I thought."

Jake came in. "What happened to your horse, Steve?"

"Took an arrow."

Without knowing why, Victoria turned around. Steve's gaze was on her. "That's Ted Garrett's out there in the lean-to."

Victoria put her hand on the table and lowered herself to the bench. She could not bring herself to ask the question.

"He was among the first to die, Vicky," Steve said quietly. "He died quickly."

There was a lump in her throat. "And—the others?"

"They're dead. All of them." Steve slumped back on the bed. "There was little time for them to suffer. That's all that mattered."

His cool acceptance angered her at that moment like nothing before had. "All that mattered? You have the guts to lay there and tell me that?"

She advanced on him, unaware of Jake watching them from the fireplace or the cup trembling in her hand. "What kind of man are you? We were your responsibility! You took money. To see us safely through to El Paso. And you're relieved there was little time to suffer!"

Before she realized what she was doing, she tossed the remaining coffee in the cup over Steve. In one movement he rose from the bed and grabbed her wrist. The cup shattered on the floor.

His eyes were like shards of glass. "I might remind you that all of you elected to go against my advice. But for their own pigheadedness, they'd be alive today."

"Oh, you're good with words, Steve." They faced each other, only inches apart. The anger blazed between them like gunfire. "Next you're going to tell me that you stayed to help protect your charges!"

"All right, what are you implying?" He released her and sat on the bed, his long legs sprawled out before him. She knew that, weakened by the wound, his strength was ebbing. "What's eating at you, Vicky?"

"Ted's horse. Ted's horse was at the back—tied to my wagon. Or rather, *your* wagon full of rifles. Admit it, Steve. The only reason you had to return to the rear of the wagon train was for your precious guns. Blood money! Isn't that what you call a mercenary's pay?"

"You got a bitchy little mind, Victoria Romero. Or should I call you the Widow Garrett?"

"How dare you even mention his name. You!" She sputtered in helpless fury. "You caused all their deaths. Our guide! Why, you're nothing but a murderer!"

"You play the part of the bereaved widow quite convincingly, Vicky. Funny, though. I didn't notice you protecting your helpless husband while the Mescaleros— Oh, what the hell!" He reached down next to the bed and shoved the saddlebag so that it slid across the floor at her feet. "It was Ted's. Yours now. Take it and get out."

"You're both full of more crap than a Christmas turkey!" Jake said. "She ain't going nowhere till the Mescaleros have cleared out." He turned to her. "And you, missy. You oughta get your facts straight 'fore you decide to play judge and jury."

Victoria and Steve glared at each other like wary cocks, disappointed that they were temporarily restrained from tearing at each others' throats. But both of them well knew the inevitable moment would come.

"I'm going out," she said between clenched teeth. "I need some fresh air."

She stumbled over the saddlebag, and she heard Steve laugh. "Oh, you—you—"

"I know, I know," he said, falling back on the bed. "You've already told me what I am."

Victoria grabbed up the bags and stomped out. Behind the cabin was a creek. Midafternoon sunlight streamed through the pines as she walked down the slight incline and took a seat along the mossy bank.

207

Beneath her spread skirts was a carpet of pine needles. The air was fresh with the scent of wild berries. As she sat there, her arms wrapped about her knees, she found it hard to believe that only the day before, the massacre of people she had lived with—and loved—had taken place not fifty miles away.

The painful memory reminded her of the saddlebags at her side. Ted's saddlebags. Or hers now, as Steve had so callously reminded her.

Curious yet hesitant about going through the articles that had been a part of Ted's life, Victoria at last unbuckled one bag and raised the flap with the U.S. Army insignia stamped on it. Her mouth dropped open. There were stacks of money inside. U.S. currency. Not believing her eyes, she began counting the stacks. Four hundred dollars!

On her knees now, she opened the other bag, rapidly thumbing through the stacks it contained. Five hundred dollars. Nearly one thousand in all! Now she knew why Ted had been so concerned about Rider, not wanting anyone near his horse. This was the money he had been saving for his eventual return to Virginia.

For a moment she sat back, stunned, not believing it was hers. She thought of the prospects that lay in the future for her; the doors that would be opened, the wishes that could come true; the goals she could finally gain. Ruefully she put the bound stacks back in the bags. Six hours as Ted Garrett's wife, she felt, did not make the money hers, regardless of what the law said.

Dejectedly, she hoisted the bags over her shoulder and started back for the cabin. Inside, Steve was asleep. Jake sat at the table cleaning his gun. "Jake," she asked, closing the door softly behind her, "did you know what was in Ted's saddlebags?"

"Yes'm," he said, never turning around.

She went over to him. "Jake, I'm not entitled to this money. Can you tell me how to find Ted's relatives? Surely the military would have records. Could I look at them?"

"You could, but seems pretty foolhardy to me. If Lieutenant Garrett wanted to marry you bad enough he'd get out of his sickbed, then I'd sure think he'd want to share his . . . wealth with you." Jake looked around at her. "Hear tell his family back east is rich. Appears you could use the money more than them."

Victoria nodded, wanting desperately to believe Jake was right. Why, she wondered, did a person have to feel guilty when some good fortune came her way which she did not necessarily earn?

It was silly, she told herself. When setbacks had faced her, she had never thought of giving up, yet let some fantastic event like this happen, and she was ready to chuck it all.

Steve awoke a little later that evening. Belligerently, she took him the left-over bowl of beans, saying nothing, and returned to the table to finish her own bowl. It was a quiet meal, all of them still remembering the battle that had raged in the cabin earlier.

As night came, and neither of the men spoke about where Victoria was to sleep, she started wondering what they had in mind. It seemed to her they both assumed she would share the bed with Steve. When Jake rolled up in a buffalo robe before the fireplace, she stalked to the bed and whipped off one of the animal furs. As she wrapped it about her, curling on the table top, she heard Steve chuckle.

It was a long night, and she ached to climb into the other half of the bed. But pride kept her from doing it. The next morning Jake left to go hunting, and the silence between Steve and herself hung heavy as wood smoke in the air. She knew Steve was waiting for her to say something, and she was all the more determined to ignore him.

But she could not. She could feel those eyes on her, compelling and uncompromising. Finally, she could stand it no longer. "I'm going to wash up," she said. She took a towel from one of the pegs and hurried from the cabin before Steve could say anything.

The rushing mountain stream was frigid, but she knelt on its bank resolutely and began washing away the grit and grime that had accumulated in the long dull strands for more than a week. When she had scrubbed her face and neck, she combed the tangles from her hair with a comb she had found in the cabin. She noted one of the teeth was missing, and she found it difficult to think of Steve being an ordinary man, using a comb with a broken tooth.

When the sun had dried her tresses to their natural blue-black sheen so that the curls feathered at the ends with a life of their own, Victoria reluctantly returned to the cabin.

His eyes opened as she shut the door behind her, as if he knew her thoughts had been on him. She put the comb and towel away and moved about the room on various pretexts.

After a while Steve said, "Vicky, come here."

"What do you want?"
"Are you afraid of me?"
"That's one day you'll never see!"
"Then come here."

XX

✬✬✬✬✬✬✬✬✬✬

Slowly she moved forward until her skirts touched the bedside. "Well?" she asked, looking down into the green, fathomless eyes.

He took her hand and pulled her down so that she sat beside his long frame stretched out there. "You've fought me all the way. Since that first day you tried to kill me at Rose's. And it's time we cleared it all up. I want to know why."

She pressed her lips together.

"Damn it, Vicky. You might hate me, but at least be honest. Or is honesty something you don't understand?"

Victoria bristled and tried to jerk her hand away, but he held it firmly. "What is it, Vicky? Why the hate?"

How could she tell him what she did not understand herself? Steve waited patiently.

"You're right, Steve—about not understanding."

"I think you're afraid to understand." His voice was level, yet she knew there was a pressure building beneath it, the same building inside her. Did she fear the explosion, she wondered; the confrontation that was irrevocably bound to occur?

"No! Oh, I don't know. I don't understand it exactly—what it is that drives me to hate you like I do. Oh, I had reason to dislike your kind. You were a *Diablo Tejano*."

Steve raised one brow.

"You—I mean the Texas Rangers—rode into my town when I was younger. I watched them perform feats of savagery . . . sometimes I think worse feats than any Indian could."

At that moment it was as if she were back there in the dusty streets. The hideous Texas yell. The sight of the Mexican farmer hanging from a signpost. The little brown boy running barefoot through the street, stumbling suddenly under bright gunfire. The warm, sticky blood between her legs.

She knew she was trembling, but she could not stop. Steve raised one swarthy hand and pushed back her tumbled hair, continuing to stroke the soft, gleaming curls until the trembling stopped.

She looked down into his face, dark and quiet and intent. "You call the Indians savage because you're supposed to be civilized. But your veneer of civiliza-

214

tion—it didn't stop your kind from killing my brother. It didn't stop your kind from raping me. So when I saw you asleep that afternoon at Rose's, I didn't stop to think. Can you blame me, Steve? You represented all I hate . . . all the hurt!"

She did not realize her words were tumbling out until Steve wiped a tear from her cheek. "Go on, Vicky."

"Then—when you mistook me for one of Rose's girls and used me like that—so coldly, so ruthlessly— the hate began to eat away at me. If you can really call it hate. Sometimes—dear God—I think the hate's greater than I can bear!"

Steve pulled her down against his good shoulder. "Shhh, *corazón*. It's all right. It's all right."

He took her chin in one hand, forcing her to look at him. "Vicky, will you forgive me?"

His voice was husky with suppressed emotion. "How was I to know you weren't one of Rose's girls? What can I say—except that right now I'm not even sorry it happened. Because I wouldn't have known—*Dios mio*, how I want you!"

Gently his lips brushed her wet cheeks, brushed her long wet lashes. Slowly his lips moved back and claimed her own. His mouth was warm, soft on hers. It was an agony for her to draw a breath, and, like a rabbit hypnotized by fear, she was unable to move.

Then, by her own volition, her lips moved beneath his, welcoming the sensation his parted lips conveyed. She was surprised. By the pleasure—by her own reaction. She made no protest as he pulled her against him so that their bodies lay lengthwise.

He began to make love to her with incredible tenderness, giving totally even as he took. But even in that giving, his passion grew more demanding, and even in her resistance she felt she was losing herself. For before, she had managed to remain apart from the violation of her body. Before, she had withdrawn, divorced herself from the degrading actions. But now she had no control over herself, over her own passions that rose to meet his. His lips scalded her, and his burning hands coaxed her to greater heights. They cupped her breasts as his fiery tongue traced patterns about her nipples, then moved lower, raking a path of pain and pleasure to her belly. A half-scream, half-moan mingled with her rapid breathing as his fingers found her.

She began to shake violently, an unknown fear crowding out all other emotion. She stood on the threshold of some mind-rending discovery—and she was afraid. Afraid of submission, afraid of being nothing more than the tool of another's will, the pawn of another's whim.

"No!" she cried out, shrinking from Steve's embrace. He looked at her questioningly, his probing eyes inescapable.

"I think you are a coward, Vicky," he whispered.

"Steve," she begged, "you don't understand."

He rolled to a sitting position. Calmly he took a thin piece of paper from his shirt pocket and emptied a small amount of tobacco on it from the tin he carried.

Finally, after he had lit the cigarette, he looked down at her and said, "Are you trying to avoid the payment due me?"

It was like a slap in the face. Stiffly, she rose from the bed. "I'm glad you reminded me. In a moment of weakness I had almost forgotten how mercenary you are. But I promise you, Steve Kaptain, that's something I'll never give you of my own free will."

He smiled, but his eyes were cold and impersonal. "Then shall I force you?"

"I don't think you're in any condition right now to force me."

"For once I agree with you. But the time will come when I'll collect my payment. And you will give it— just as passionately as you wanted to only moments ago."

His words were clipped and cold, but his long lips, which even at that moment Victoria found difficult to draw her gaze from, parted in a self-assured, knowing smile.

She would have thrown herself on him, scratching him, marking him on the outside as he had marked her on the inside, had not Jake entered then. If he noticed Victoria's dishevelment, he made no comment. In one hand was the skinned carcass of a squirrel. "I hope you two are hungry, 'cause I went to a lot of trouble to get this measly thing."

Neither Steve nor she spoke.

It was not until after supper that the atmosphere seemed to lose some of its tenseness. Steve was strong enough to leave the bed and sit with Jake before the fireplace, coffee cups and cigarettes in their hands, while Victoria washed the dishes. The two of them discussed in low voices the deal she remembered Jake mentioning at Brandt's trading post.

"Half the money's yours," Steve said. "I want you to take my share with you. Buy out Kenedy and King. Those riverboats'll control the trade on both sides of the entire Rio Grande one day."

217

"Could be a good investment," Jake said, his eyes squinted as if trying to read the future. "If Legs Lewis don't beat us to it."

"That's why I want you to leave tomorrow—or the day after at the latest. Legs was up at Caddo last I heard. But he could have beat a trail down to Fort Brown by this time."

Steve paused, and Victoria heard him add, "And I want you to take her with you."

XXI

✠✠✠✠✠✠✠✠✠✠✠

Victoria stood on the bare hilltop with the Rio Grande twisting like a snake below, deep there because of the gorge that hemmed it in. On the other side of the river was the limitless stretch of Mexico's white desert and purple mountains. Her homeland.

Behind her was the collection of shanties, built, because of the scarcity of timber, of sunbaked bricks or rough layered rocks and roofed by grass thatch or matting packed hard with earth.

In the harsh, late afternoon sun it was a dismal sight, but all the same those huts represented civilization to Victoria. Thirteen days of hard, breakneck riding, never once seeing a white man other than Jake—or even an elusive Indian—brought her to that desolate town, Rio Grande City. And yet she hoped, beyond all reason, that the sight of other faces would dispel the desperate loneliness, the hurt, the bitterness that made her present life miserable.

Jake was at her elbow. "Gabe says the *Corvette* isn't due in till tomorrow."

"What will we do until then?"

"Most folks use Gabe's place as a layover. He doesn't charge much for bed and a meal."

Money was no longer a worry for Victoria, but she took up the horse's reins, Ted's horse, and tiredly followed Jake back to the cluster of huts. At the door a shabbily dressed, barefoot woman watched them. Her yellow hair hung untidily about her thin face.

The woman, Jake called her Betsy, moved aside to let them pass. "Gabe says you'll be wanting supper," she said surlily. "All we got is beans and 'taters."

"Suits me fine," Jake said and went over and stretched out on one of the three mattressless beds that crowded the room.

Inside, the semidark room was slovenly. It wasn't just the earthen-packed floor. It was the stale, hot air. It was the unkempt look of things lying about, the food-stained pans and crumbled clothes. It was the dust. Victoria could imagine how much worse the place would have looked had there been a window to let the daylight in, and was glad it would be only the one night she need spend there.

They had ridden at a grueling pace throughout that day, afraid they would miss the steamboat, and both were exhausted. Especially Jake, for, from the time they had left, he had been constantly alert for the marauding Mescaleros. Now that they had the guns from the wagon train, he believed there would be little to restrain them from all-out war with the white settlers in that area.

Victoria was tired, too. But in a different way. She was tired of thinking. Of trying, in all that had happened, to decipher the truth from lies, reality from illusion. Somewhere in the labyrinth of distortion she knew lay the answer she looked for.

Wearily she slung her saddlebags on top of the hardwood bed. Betsy turned to her, her face pinched with dislike and suspicion. Victoria could see her small mind working, wondering what Victoria was to Jake—and Steve, for surely, Victoria thought, Steve had been there too. Had the drab frontierswoman in her dirty calico dress also fallen under Steve's charm, she wondered. Suddenly she felt sorry for Betsy.

"Don't got no place for you to wash up."

"It doesn't matter," Victoria told her, sitting on the other bed and removing her black, flat-crowned hat so that it hung by its cords on her back.

Victoria could imagine how she looked. Even wearing the broad-brimmed hat had not protected her complexion. Looking at the backs of her hands, she knew she was as brown as any Indian. And she had lost all her pins sometime during the second day of hard riding, so that now she wore her hair loose. How Steve would ridicule her if he could see her now!

"Jake, where's your bottle of whiskey?"

Jake eyed her curiously. After a minute he said, "It's gone, missy. Betsy, get the lady a bottle of mescal and a glass."

The woman dug out a bottle from a rickety cupboard and stonily handed it to Victoria along with a chipped glass that looked as if, like Betsy's hair, it could use a good washing.

Victoria sat the glass on the hard-packed floor and settled back against the musty wall, the bottle cradled in one hand. Disregarding Jake's watchful stare, she proceeded to drink the bitter liquid. At that moment she did not care what Jake thought. He had already told her what he thought—the only time there had been a chance to talk in that harrowing two week flight.

"You're mighty muleheaded 'bout something you ain't one hundred percent sure 'bout." he had said over one of the few campfires he had permitted them.

"I don't know what you're talking about, Jake."

" 'Bout Steve. You done decided he's wrong without giving him a chance to defend himself."

"It wouldn't matter. Steve Kaptain would never bother to defend himself. Because he doesn't give a damn what anyone thinks . . . or feels."

"Then I got something to say, missy. It wasn't the guns Steve returned for back there at Salt Draw."

Across the flickering flames of the campfire Victoria looked up sharply at Jake.

"You didn't think those guns were Steve's, did you?" he asked. "Brandt and Garrett were making money by selling them to the Indians."

"I don't believe you. Steve—Steve himself told me he had arranged with Brandt to sell those guns to the people at San Elizario."

"Beg your pardon, missy. But that was most likely just to keep you quiet. Steve didn't want any questions asked. You see, missy, Steve never was supposed to be the wagon train's guide. The train could have found itself some old Indian scout. But the Army—it was alarmed at the Indian attacks on the settlers—mostly, Mescalero Apaches—with guns. What happened, after some investigating, was the Army noticed that Garrett had managed to pull frontier duty some eight times over the past three years. And during several of the duties there was reportings of Indians with guns. It was Steve's job to keep an eye on this shipment of guns. Brandt thought Garrett had brought Steve in on the deal, and vice-versa. Garrett probably hoped to unload them somewhere around the Pecos. Probably would have, if a snake bite hadn't stopped him."

"You're saying that this money," she indicated the saddlebags, "that it was made from the sale of the guns? That it's blood money?"

"No, ma'am, I ain't. The Army wouldn't be able to prove where it came from. When the Indians couldn't trade their furs or stolen horses for firearms, they'd take cash, and then find someone else willing to sell them the firearms for the cash."

"Someone like Ted," Victoria had whispered, still not quite believing, not wanting to believe.

Victoria took another swallow of the mescal and choked before finally getting the harsh brew down. If Jake was right, she thought, then Ted had been lying to her. All the eloquent words about how he had applied for duty to be near her.

And Steve—he had been just as deceiving. Lie after lie he had piled up. How he had arranged with Brandt for her to ride with the train; informing the Army she was his cook, a camp follower; letting her believe he was rescuing her from a murder charge when all the time the charge had been dropped.

Unsteadily, she put the half-empty bottle down, the distaste in her mouth more for all men in general than for Gabe's poor-quality mescal. "To hell with Steve Kaptain and all men!" she thought, laying her head on her saddlebags and falling asleep.

The long, mellow blast of a whistle awoke her the next morning. Her head ached, and she flinched each time the steamboat whistle announced its coming. Cautiously, she opened her eyes against the sunlight streaming through the doorway.

Jake stood framed there by the sunlight. "*Corvette*'s here, missy. Get your bags, they're loading up."

Victoria struggled to her feet with the saddlebags, and sharp waves of nausea assailed her stomach. There was a first time for everything, she thought, and drinking herself into forgetfulness would also be the last time.

Outside, the sun beat unmercifully on her head, and she hurriedly put on her wide-brim hat. Jake eyed her but said nothing. On both sides of the Rio Grande people had gathered to watch the *Corvette* dock. It lay tied there at the landing, blowing off steam, its big paddle wheel idle.

Victoria and Jake edged through the raggedly clothed farmers and peons and the excited children. The two made their way down the steep incline to the wharf where men were unloading bolts of cotton cloth, bags of sugar, and boxes of hardware. Others were bringing on board wool, hides, and fruits and vegetables.

"How be ye, Jake?"

Victoria looked up to see two men, their heads above the other men, standing on board the *Corvette*. The one who had called out wore a captain's hat. He waved his large hand to get Jake's attention.

"That's Richard King," Jake said. "An Irish Yankee and tough to boot."

Richard King was square-built and brawny, and, Victoria thought, attractive in a rough-hewn sort of way. But it was the other who drew her attention. Equally as tall as Richard King, he was dashingly dressed in dark broadcloth. The roguish smile in his dark face had the same quality of magnetism as did Steve's.

"Looks like Legs Lewis may have beat us to it," Jake said, his face stony below the feathered hat.

When Victoria realized the gentleman was Steve's rival for the Kenedy-King packet, her interest in the man grew.

As the two crossed the gangplank, King, his bowed legs moving like a true sailor's, came to meet them. He extended his hand to Jake. "And where be my drinking buddy, Steve?"

"On his way to Austin, Dick. Reports to file for the military."

"Oh, to be sure," King answered and turned to Victoria. His eyes, like hers, were a high-spirited blue. "And who might this beautiful colleen be?"

He moved closer and took her hands between his large, roughened ones, and Victoria noticed the slightly misshapen left nostril that made the face infectiously appealing. "I'm Victoria Garrett," she said.

"My pleasure, Mrs. Garrett," he said with a broad smile.

Behind him, she saw the man called Legs Lewis. His lids were half-closed in a lazy way, as if he was appraising her, and she found herself slightly drawn to his good looks. "May I introduce myself?" he asked, when Richard King had released her hand.

"I already know who you are, Mr. Lewis. You'd be a difficult man not to notice."

An appreciative smile appeared below the neatly clipped mustache. "I respect honesty, Miss Garrett."

"*Mrs.* Garrett, Mr. Lewis."

"Oh?" His raven-black brows lifted slightly. "And where is the lucky man that has claimed your hand and heart?"

Her eyes met his levelly. "My husband is dead," she answered, keeping her voice emotionless.

"Then let me be equally honest, Victoria," he said, using her first name as if they had been close friends for a long time. "For your sake, I'm sorry . . . but as for myself, I'm delighted to learn you are a widow."

Victoria smiled, quite caught up by the man's charm.

"I hate to interrupt your courtship, Legs," Dick said pleasantly, "but why don't we let the passengers remove to their cabins? Mrs. Garrett," he said, facing her with a merry smile, "I didn't expect to have a lady aboard, but pleased I'd be if you'd have my cabin for the return journey."

"Will the trip take long?" she asked.

"We shall be in Fort Brown within six days, ma'am, or my steamboat isn't the best west of the Mississippi." He turned back to Jake. "We can get down to negotiations at dinner, mate. Right now, I got to check the provisions lists."

Victoria found Captain King's quarters to be a little cabin with a hardwood floor bare of rugs, a small desk with papers strewn across it, a round table, and a bunk. It was for the bunk she headed, intending to sleep off her first hangover, until dinner that evening. The rhythmic slapping of the water against the shallow-draft steamboat lulled her to sleep at once.

By dinnertime she was famished. The sleep had restored her, although she feared there was little to help her looks. She glanced in the cracked mirror and tried to comb her tangled hair with her fingers. She bit her lips for some color.

Legs, Dick, and Jake were already outside on the deck waiting for her. "You'll have to forgive me, gentlemen, for my dress," she said with a regretful half-smile, indicating her brown rumpled skirt and travel-stained long-sleeved blouse. "Jake may have told you that we lost everything—in an Indian raid on the wagon train we were with."

"Everything but our scalps," Jake added grimly.

Legs's wickedly dark eyes raked over Victoria with admiration. He offered her his arm, saying, "I know just the place in Fort Brown to shop for clothing, Victoria. Madame Gautier, a creole out of New Orleans, owns a clothing shop. She's a good friend. Will you allow me to introduce you to her when we arrive?"

Victoria flashed a glance at Jake, knowing Steve had ordered him to take her back to Reynosa.

Dick interrupted, his laugh hearty. "Be careful, Mrs. Garrett, that's all he introduces you to. Oh, Legs is welcome in all the higher circles," Dick hastened to explain with a smile, "but he be quite notorious for his pastime—gambling."

227

They stepped inside a narrow hallway which opened into a large room. In its center was a long wooden table secured to the floor. When Legs had seated Victoria, and the others had taken their places, Legs said, "I'm not bluffing about the packet deal, Dick. I can write you a draft on my New Orleans bank now."

Dick looked sheepishly at Jake, who as yet had said nothing. "Indeed, I be interested, Legs. But to be fair Steve and Jake got first bid."

Jake removed his hat. "We're prepared to offer two hundred—in cash. And from the sale of the rest of the Sierra Diablo cattle we can raise another three."

"I'll go higher," Legs said calmly. "Seven hundred."

"Cash?" Jake asked.

Legs gazed at Jake expressionlessly for several seconds before turning to Dick. "Well, Dick," he asked, drawing deep on the cigar held between his long, immaculate fingers, "what's it to be?"

Dick frowned with indecision. He rose and poured each of them a sherry from the decanter on the hutch. When he returned with the four glasses held gingerly in his big hands, he said, "Jake, I know Legs's credit be good. Miflin and me need the money for my ranch venture at Santa Gertruda."

Jake tipped his chair on its back legs and thought a minute. "Understand you, Dick. We want the packet, but we can't swing seven hundred right now."

Legs took one of the glasses from Dick and raised it in a toast toward Jake. "In all my years playing poker against Steve Kaptain, I've never beat him. I believe my luck's changing. Here's to a new beginning."

"One grand." Victoria's voice rang clear in the paneled cabin.

The three men turned toward her with startled expressions.

"I bid one thousand, Dick."

She looked at Jake. "That is, if Jake would be willing to take five hundred dollars cash and me as a silent third partner."

Jake gazed at the amber liquid in his glass. "I don't know, missy, that I can rightly speak for us without Steve's approval."

Victoria had never played poker, but she had watched others. She sat there, a bland expression on her face.

Legs said, "One thousand one hundred, Dick."

"Twelve hundred," she countered.

Dick looked at Jake. Jake nodded his head. "You've won, colleen," Dick said. "Looks like you, Jake, and Steve—along with a small shareholder, Charles Stillman, be the new proprietors of the *Corvette*."

Victoria picked up her glass. "I believe with my seven hundred that makes me the controlling partner of the venture, doesn't it, gentlemen?"

"I believe, Victoria," Legs said, "I have finally met my match . . . a beautiful lady with a head on her shoulders."

Victoria's smile was mystical, for she was remembering an old man, Dr. Ricktor, who had said the same thing of her in Rose's office. It all seemed so long ago. "Thank you for the compliment. Should we toast to our new venture, gentlemen?"

All three men rose in unison and lifted their glasses, but rather than as a toast to the new venture, it was a tribute to the warm beauty and intelligent wit of the woman who stood before them. A very desirable woman with her blue eyes flashing like sapphires and her inky-black hair spilling over her shoulders.

"Before you lose your head, Legs," Dick said, "if you're still interested in making an investment, Miflin and me could use more capital in the Santa Gertruda acquisition."

"Are you sure you're not Scottish, Richard King?" Legs asked, displaying his charming smile.

After dinner Legs walked Victoria around the deck, which was crowded with the new cargo that had been taken on at the Davis landing in Rio Grande City and the boilers and engine, which emitted the smell of still-hot oil. In the twilight the Rio Grande looked serene, its waters a deep blue, not the dirty brown they were by day.

Victoria was intensely interested in her newly acquired business, the first thing she had ever owned, and Legs attentively explained to her its workings. From the basics that steamboats do not travel at night because of the danger of ramming into snags—the drifts and bars that are hidden in the water—to the advice she should sell out her share within five years.

"The westward march of the railroads will eventually drive the steamboats from the waterways," he said, a melancholy expression on his darkly handsome face.

Victoria ran her hand along the gingerbread ornamentation of the railing, feeling linked with Legs through their mutual fondness for the steamboat.

He tossed his cigar overboard. "Victoria," he said, taking her firmly by the shoulders, "I've been called a rake and a lot of other things, but men have always taken my word as a gentleman. For that same reason,

I've never married. After a while, I knew I'd become bored and I'd start looking around for other— pleasures. And I would not be the type to hide my philandering. Rather than also be called a cheat and a liar I chose not to marry . . . until now."

For a moment Victoria was tempted to play the coquette, but she at last said, "That sounds like a proposal, Legs."

"It is," he said with a twinkle in his black eyes. "And if you'd like, I'll go down on one knee and tell you that your eyes are as blue as the Gulf at dawn and your tresses are as lovely as sable fur and—" He drew her close to him and whispered against her hair. "And it would give me incredible pleasure to show you what love is really like."

Victoria drew away from him slightly. "You are direct, aren't you?"

Legs took both her hands in his and kissed them lightly. "I'm sorry if I offended you, Victoria. You're a mysterious woman that I want to know—and have for my own. I'm afraid that, like gambling, you're going to become a passion with me."

"I hope not," she said sincerely. "The stakes aren't worth it."

"I'll take that chance. Will you give me an answer? Will you marry me?"

"I'm—I'm honored by your proposal—because I admire you greatly, Legs. And I'm sure any female would be wild to trap you, but . . ." she let her voice drift off.

"But your heart belongs to someone else? Is that it?"

"No," she answered sharply. "I have no heart, Legs. It was torn out a long time ago."

Legs watched her, waiting for an explanation. But when she turned her head away, looking out over the water, he shrugged. "Should you change your mind, Victoria, my proposal still stands."

XXII

✤✤✤✤✤✤✤✤✤✤✤

The *Corvette* made its way down the crooked, snaggy Rio Grande to Reynosa, where Steve had ordered Jake to leave off Victoria. But when it docked for an hour of loading, she did not disembark.

She stood at the railing, looking out over the growing but still crude and wild border town. The hot and dusty town where it first began for her—that first confrontation between herself and Steve. Since then, their paths had intertwined so many times and in so many ways that she thought their two lives resembled a raveled and knotted ball of yarn.

Like the crafty fox that has ensnared its prey, Victoria experienced the satisfaction of knowing that the tables had turned. It was she now who had control of Steve's future, no matter how small; although she still could not comfortably justify her motive for bidding on the steamboat. True, she had sensed it would be a good investment. But it was more than that. She had hoped to thwart Steve, but unreasonably she felt no triumph in having the last word.

Now, instead of Reynosa, her home would be Brownsville, the town Charles Stillman had established outside Fort Brown. Here were the head offices of Miflin Kenedy and Richard King's steamboat company. And here she would begin again. She smiled thinly when she thought of the fact that she would at last have the luxuries of wealth that she had done without since childhood. It was true that she did not have an established name that would enable her to quickly gain society's ranks. But society's calling card would wait. She was in no hurry.

Midmorning of the sixth day brought the *Corvette* in sight of the twin cities at the mouth of the Rio Grande. The three men and Victoria leaned on the railing, watching the cotton fields pass; they lay on both sides up and down the river.

The prettier of the two cities was Mexico's Matamoros, a town with a population of seven thousand. It stood on a level plain in the midst of palms, papayas, bougainvillea, and rich fields of orchid gardens. Out of this greenery rose the unfinished plaster spires of the cathedral.

Yet it was the raw town of Brownsville that attracted her. It was new, with less than three thousand inhabitants, room for people to grow. It was the opportunity Victoria had been looking for.

Dick had told her Brownsville was largely Mexican, but dominated and controlled by the Americans. There were also many French firms. Originally agents for New Orleans houses of commerce or with creole connections, these merchants, along with Yankee sea captains and foreign service representatives had migrated to Fort Brown, named in honor of Major Jacob Brown who died defending the fort in the Mexican-American War. In addition, many of the soldiers stationed at the fort found the exotic climate worth returning to. All had come in hopes of participating in some way in the city's fast-growing commerce, in grasping the opportunities that were opening in that virgin country.

As the *Corvette* neared the town, shopfronts and warehouses became visible. In the distance the Lone Star Flag and the Stars and Stripes whipped about in the wind. Legs took Victoria aside. "I'm going to give you your first lesson in politics."

Victoria looked up into that roguish face, not believing Legs was serious. "I'm not joking, Victoria. Since you don't intend to marry me—for the moment anyway—I can only conclude you intend to make your own way—with your investment to back you."

She nodded.

"Then I shall proceed with the summation of Brownsville's political affairs—in which you shall, I am most certain, become involved."

"Me?"

"Yes, you. You see, there are two political factions in Brownsville, both controlled by Americans. The Red faction is controlled by Charles Stillman—yes, he's the one who still holds a small interest in your newly acquired steamboat. Some years ago he bought up a large tract of land adjoining Fort Brown and formed a company which established the townsite of Brownsville. Arbitrarily, he named several city streets for his family—Elizabeth for his wife, St. Francis for his father, and"—Legs smiled wryly—"St. Charles for himself."

"He sounds quite conceited."

"At one time he was also considered ruthless. But I doubt he'll be a thorn in your side. His health is failing, and he's expected to sell his share to an old friend. It's the leader of the Blue faction, the mayor, you should be concerned with—Matthew Farrington."

Laughing, Victoria held up a small hand of protest. "You're going a little fast for me, Legs."

He took her hand. "Just wait until I finish explaining. Matthew Farrington has enjoyed the confidence of Martin Van Buren and served under him as minister to Switzerland. When Texas became a state, Matthew was shrewd enough to realize that the city on the northern side of the Rio Grande, Brownsville, would flourish, controlling all the trade of northern Mexico and rivaling Galveston and New Orleans for the Gulf trade."

Legs pointed to the river front of Matamoros. "Most of the warehouses you see there are his. They are used for storing contraband. If you hope to succeed here, Victoria, I would not cross him."

"Is he as formidable as you make him out to be?"

"More so. He's in the prime of life, with no family to distract him from his commercial empire—which is all of South Texas. He has a hand in every pot. Land developer, ranch owner, merchant. He's just as arrogant and cold-blooded as Stillman used to be. But Matthew is fair. You see, until he took office, there were two different sets of law here—one for the political leaders and the prominent Americans and the other for the lower classes and the old landholding Mexican families."

"And you, Legs? Which side do you belong to?"

"Neither. A gambler always takes the middle of the fence—and you should, too."

"Your description of the man makes him highly intriguing, but I doubt our paths shall cross."

"I seriously hope not," Legs said, planting a light kiss on each of Victoria's hands before releasing them. "For I would hate to challenge the man to a duel over you."

Victoria laughed gaily, never suspecting the dominant role Matthew Farrington was to play in her immediate future.

Dick remained behind to oversee the unloading while Legs, Jake, and Victoria made their way along the street that fronted the Rio Grande. There, Legs hired a carriage to take them to the Miller Hotel.

Jake declined the ride. "Got friends at the Fort that'll put me up."

Victoria reached out her hand and took his callused one. "Jake, I appreciate everything you've done for me."

Jake's voice was gruff. " 'Twarn't nothing, missy. Good luck in your life here."

"Will I see you again?"

"I doubt it. Samuel Belden, a lawyer here, will most likely handle our end of the business. If you need anything, see him."

She watched him go with mixed emotions. She would miss the old scout, but she was relieved that she would not have to face Steve again. She knew that, in addition to everything else that made her fear him, he would be furious with her for meddling in his business.

The carriage turned down Washington Street, and Legs pointed out the Stillman House, the pride of Brownsville, explaining it was the only house there with Southern Colonial architecture. It had been built of native hand-made brick, and Stillman had imported real New England slate shingles.

Everywhere were Texas Rangers. In the shops, along the streets, even in the hotels—their spurs jingling on their boots, rifles in their hands, Colt revolvers in their holsters, and bowie knives tucked into their belts.

"What are those Rangers doing here?" she asked.

"The citizens of Brownsville petitioned the state for two Ranger companies to protect them from the Mexican and Indian raids. At one time I was a Ranger myself."

"I should have known."

He looked at her steadily. "Why the mysterious remark?"

Victoria put out a placating hand. "I didn't mean it to sound that way, Legs. It's just that the Texas Ranger has in one way or another been a part of my life since I was a small girl. I know the mere sight of a Texas Ranger used to bring terror—maybe it still does."

She was surprised that she could talk so calmly about something that had left such deep marks on her. Legs put a comforting arm about Victoria's shoulders.

"If you'd let me, Victoria, I'd give you both my name and my protection . . . so you'd never have to fear anything again."

Victoria looked down at her clasped hands, and Legs said, "You don't have to answer that until you're ready." And then on a lighter note, "But you don't have to worry about them." He nodded in the direction of several Rangers. "Rip Ford keeps them pretty well under control."

"He's here? Do you know Rip?"

"My service with Rip taught me to read men. An invaluable aid in poker. You can never know a man, Victoria, until you've made a scout with him in bad weather. Rip'll tell you that all the good qualities and bad force their way to the surface when a man is suffering from privation and danger."

"If you have such a high esteem for the Rangers, why'd you quit?"

Legs smiled wickedly. "I decided there was a better way to make a living."

The carriage passed Market House, an impressive two-story building with open arches and high cupolas, and halted in front of Miller Hotel on the opposite side of the crowded public square.

Dressed in the same clothes she had worn for more than three weeks, Victoria dreaded entering the hotel along with the elegantly dressed men and women. But she lifted her square chin proudly and took the arm Legs offered.

He flashed her a reassuring smile. "You're the most beautiful woman in Brownsville," he whispered at her ear. "And after you meet Madame Gautier, you'll be the best-dressed. I'll come by for you tomorrow morning and take you there."

"You won't be staying here?"

His smile was as cryptic as hers had been earlier. "When I'm in Brownsville, I stay at quarters in an older section of the town."

Victoria felt it wise not to question him further. They parted at the hotel desk, where Legs procured a room for her before kissing her hand in the European manner and taking his leave.

Victoria's room was richly furnished, and she ran her hand over the Victorian hand-carved, four-poster maple bed with delight. When she was a child there had been such a bed in her room at the hacienda. It was difficult for her to believe she would sleep in something so luxurious once again.

True to his word, Legs came by for her early the next morning. Not far from the hotel, on a side street, was Madame Gautier's shop. There were several ladies already inside, but the plump woman rapidly dispersed them when she saw Legs.

"Legs, you *enfant terrible*! Where have you been?" A heavily rouged woman of middle age, she crossed the room in short, rapid steps. "On another escapade, no doubt. And who is this?" she asked, withdrawing her hand before Legs could kiss it.

"This is—"

"No, wait, *chéri*. Don't tell me. This must be Madame Garrett."

"But how did you know?" Victoria asked, startled.

"She knows everything." Legs said. with a wry smile. "Though how, I can't imagine. She never gives anyone else a chance to talk."

Madame Gautier took Victoria's hand and patted it. "I don't need to ask questions about this *charmeuse*. All of Brownsville is discussing her, Legs. A beautiful woman with a tragic past mysteriously appears. Not only is she wealthy, she owns part of Brownsville's most important commercial property. Who wouldn't talk, *mon fils*, about one such as this?"

"Please," Victoria said, putting out a restraining hand. "You're embarrassing me."

"La, child. Don't ever be embarrassed. You must act as *haute* and regal as a queen. I predict you're going to rule this outpost of Anglo-American civilization within the month."

She pulled Victoria toward the window where the warm morning sun streamed in. "You're far too short," she said, her painted eyes running over the young woman critically. "But you're small-boned, small-waisted, and have enough bosom to wear my creations well. Of course, my designs are not inexpensive, madame."

"That isn't important," Legs said, before Victoria could reply. "And now I'll leave you two women alone." He gave Madame Gautier a peck on the temple and, reminding Victoria he would return in the hour, took his leave.

"Now, *chérie*," the older woman said, "we must get to work. With that incredible shade of blue eyes, we shall add just a hint of indigo above the lids. But your hair!" She grimaced. "However, it is an unusual color. Black as soot. My nephew, Jean, will be able to style it in no time."

Madame Gautier fluffed Victoria's hair with her small, rounded hands. "I think your hair would look becoming piled in ringlets atop your head and held in

241

place by tortoise-shell combs. Yes, I'm sure it would be quite the thing."

When Legs returned, Victoria felt like another person. She left the shop dressed in a pert cornflower-blue gown with short, sloping sleeves and rows of lace trimming. Someone had neglected to pick up the dress, and Madame Gautier let her have it for a price, the woman assured her, that was very reasonable. She promised Victoria that the rest of the gowns, six in all, would be delivered at the end of the week.

Gingerly balancing the boxes of shoes, hats, gloves, and delicately laced underwear, Legs helped Victoria into the carriage. "I've arranged for us to have lunch at Pierre's," he said. "Pierre Ballier's another European, who has turned a profit with his French cuisine."

Victoria found Pierre's to be an intimate restaurant decorated with flowery plants and lush shrubbery artfully placed. The room was filled with people, mostly men, wearing the latest fashion in dress and exuding an atmosphere of sophistication. From all about could be heard conversations in various languages. An overtone of animation and stimulation pervaded, something Victoria had missed hungrily since coming to the frontier.

Legs's black eyes never left her, and she finally blushed. "Am I that changed?" she asked in a hushed voice.

"Yes, you know you are."

"And you do not like the change?"

He smiled ruefully. "For a while, Victoria, you have belonged solely to me. But very soon I believe I shall have to share you with the drawing rooms of Brownsville."

Victoria smiled. "You're flattering me now, Legs. I

much preferred the other gentleman—the Legs I know who is direct and honest."

Legs laughed but said, "I couldn't be more honest." He poured them both some wine and, raising his glass, said, "To your happiness, Victoria."

Midway through the lunch, she began to feel uncomfortably aware of eyes other than Legs's watching her. It was then she noticed a middle-aged gentleman, tastefully dressed in an expensively cut business suit. He was at a table toward the rear of the room with two other gentlemen. But it was he, Victoria was certain, who had been staring at her.

He rose to leave, and she noticed that, though only of medium height, he was square-set and powerfully built. His face had an intelligent forcefulness about it that caught one's attention immediately.

"Legs, who is that man there? The one with the dark brown hair?"

Legs smiled. "That, my girl, is the mayor, Matthew Farrington."

Victoria turned to watch him leave. "What's he like, Legs? I mean the person—not the businessman."

"The two are inseparable, my dear. When Matthew wants to, he can be very charming. Unfortunately, most of the time objects rather than people interest him. Power and profit are the clues to his—shall I say dynamic personality."

Legs looked at her for a moment, then said, "Is there a reason for the special interest?"

"Because he has been watching me."

"And do you wish to meet him? If so, I'll have an introduction arranged." There was a distant quality to his voice.

Victoria put her hand over his. "What is it, Legs?"

He shook his head. "Nothing, really. I was reminded of a fairy tale I heard as a boy."

"Oh? What was it?"

He smiled. "Beauty and the Beast."

"And you are implying, I take it, I am the Beauty, and the Beast is this mayor?"

"Most certainly. And as in the story, I believe you shall charm the Beast, changing him into a human again."

Victoria laughed aloud at the absurdity.

XXIII

❅❅❅❅❅❅❅❅❅❅❅❅

Legs found a small home for Victoria not far from Madame Gautier's shop. Its brick front was even with the street, and there was a narrow wrought-iron terrace on the second floor. Madame Gautier told Victoria the old lady who had owned the home had been forced to give it up because of the stairs and had gone to live with her son and his family in Point Isabel, an impoverished seaport near Brownsville.

On the same day Victoria signed the deed for the house, she signed the legal papers on the steamboat, *Corvette*, turning over a check for seven hundred to Samuel Belden, who acted as agent for both transactions. He was a burly, older man with shrewd, puffy eyes that were out of keeping with the convivial personality.

Not once did he mention Victoria's other partners—and his clients—Steve and Jake. But he did issue Legs and herself an invitation to a party being given the following week.

Belden's smile reached her from the heavy growth of graying beard. "All of Brownsville and Matamoros are anxious to meet you, Mrs. Garrett. Don Francisco Yturria of Matamoros is hosting the party, and I can promise you it will be an exciting event."

In that interval Victoria began the pleasurable task of setting up housekeeping in her first home. Legs's help was invaluable. As an eligible bachelor and most entertaining guest, every door was open to him.

He therefore knew that the quartermaster was being transferred to another post and that his wife, Mrs. Chapman, wished to sell some of their furniture. From them, Victoria bought a maple washstand with a set of pink and white china utensils, a marble-topped bedside table and bureau and a mirror framed with mother-of-pearl.

He also told her that General Wood's family had received a shipment of new furniture from England, and Victoria was able to purchase at a good price a walnut sofa and slipper chair.

From one of the shops she picked up a wooden tool chest painted dull green and a secretary desk of cherry with glass knobs.

When she was settled in, she had her first visitors, a Mrs. Bee and Miss Sims, who, she knew, had come out of avid curiosity to see what the mysterious widow was like. She offered them chocolate and, when they were leaving, promised she would soon visit them for tea at their homes.

During this time Legs was very circumspect about his visits, not wishing to bring scandal to her name. He came only twice, once to help her lower the black and white Wedgwood chandeliers, a gift of Colonel Davenport and his wife, so that Victoria could change the candles.

The day before the Yturria party, Legs sent a Mexican boy to Victoria's house with a note, telling her he would come by for her at eight the following night. His prudent respect for her caused her own feelings to grow, but never out of the bounds of a very good friendship.

The same day she hired a carriage to drive her to the bank. Belden had informed her he had deposited a check there in her account, her first month's profit as partner of the *Corvette*. It should have been an enjoyable day, but her ride was interrupted by two events.

The first was more disconcerting than startling. It was an election day. And along 13th Avenue where the polls were, tables had been set up in the street and free whiskey was being distributed. The driver of her carriage, a young Mexican man, had to swerve suddenly to avoid hitting a drunken citizen.

The second and more shocking event occurred as the carriage drove past the alley bordering the public square. Shots rang out, and a well-dressed man stumbled into view. He held his abdomen as blood gushed out over his hands. Another man came out onto the street. A revolver dangled in his hand. A crowd soon gathered around the wounded man, hampering any help that might have been offered.

"Crooked politicians!" Victoria's driver said, and spit over the wagon wheel.

"Does this sort of thing go on all the time?" she asked, mentally comparing the incident to the ones she had often seen in Reynosa.

"It's a wild, new town, *señorita*. And those politicians are the wildest of them all. Dueling with each other. All of them fighting to get to the top."

The young Mexican seemed well educated, and she said, "Why do you dislike these politicians so?"

"*Mi padre*, my father, held title to some land outside Fort Brown, near Bagdad. When some politicians found it bordered the river, they took their case to court, claiming our title was invalid because it was deeded before Texas became a state. We lost to the American lawyers. It is that way always with the old families." The young man spit again, showing his contempt.

That same afternoon Victoria posted a letter to Matthew Farrington, informing him of the two incidents and asking him how it was possible for such things to occur. She ended her letter with a description of the young Mexican driver's plight, requesting that the matter be looked into.

She did not expect anything to come of it, but the part of her that was half-Mexican rose to the surface in boiling anger at the injustice and felt some satisfaction when she had dispatched the letter.

By the following evening her anger had abated so that she was able to enjoy herself in Legs's charming company. His carriage clip-clopped across the wooden bridge that spanned the Rio Grande, the new international boundary, and entered the old-world city of Matamoros. It was a warm, tropical evening, one of those nights when romance pervades the air in the scent of orchids, jasmine, orange flowers, and lemon trees. Overhead the velvet sky was studded with diamonds.

The carriage came to a halt outside a high stucco wall where other carriages waited. Legs pulled on the bell rope, and an old, white-haired Mexican in white cotton shirt and pants swung open the grilled gate.

Inside the grounds lanterns were strung in trees and wrought-iron benches and woven chairs were placed around. There was one long table, draped in white lace, with kettles and serving dishes filled with food which wafted their aromas to the new arrivals. Many of the guests had already gathered in the open area, where *mariaches* moved among them playing romantic ballads.

"You picked a good evening to make your debut into society," Legs whispered at her side.

"Why?"

"Because I thought you might enjoy seeing two of your friends again."

Questioningly, Victoria looked up into Legs's face, close enough to him to smell the masculine odor of the men's cologne he wore.

"Rip Ford and Robert Neighbors."

"They've been invited? Where are they?"

Legs heard the pleasure in her voice, and his arm encircled her waist. "Should I be jealous? Surely both of them don't share the heart you claim not to have."

Victoria laughed, snapping her fan open to cover her amusement. "I'm surprised at your jealousy. You know

I see no one but you. And what I said, Legs, still holds true—I have no heart."

His black eyes brooded in the light of the flickering lanterns. "Yes, you've told me," he said, "but I don't believe you. Beneath that frigid exterior of yours a woman lives—waiting. And I don't believe, Victoria, it's for me."

Victoria wanted to reassure him. He had been so good to her and so good for her morale. But before she could say anything, she saw Rip coming in their direction.

"Victoria," he said, bending over her and giving her a warm kiss on the cheek, "what excitement have you brought with you this time?"

She smiled, not the least perturbed by his sly hints. She knew she could count on Rip Ford's and Robert Neighbors's discretion concerning her past. Only one had the power to ruin her forever, and, thanks to Samuel Belden, there would be no need for her to worry about Steve entering her life again—she thought.

"I believe, Rip, you're enough excitement for all of Brownsville, and the major, also. Where is he?"

"With Don Yturria," he told her. "Have you been introduced to out host and hostess yet?"

"No, we just arrived."

"That's one opportunity you won't have, Rip," Legs said. "I plan to have the privilege myself." His mouth was smiling, but his eyes mirrored a dare in their depths.

Rip bowed and smiled. "I give way to your right— this time, Legs."

Legs led Victoria to the flower-rimmed patio and introduced her to the Yturrias. While he conversed with

Don Francisco, Teresa Yturria, a brown-eyed, brown-haired woman in her twenties, said, "We've all been wanting to meet you, Señora Garrett."

"Am I that much of a *curiosidad*?" Victoria asked, returning the young woman's friendly smile.

Teresa Yturria gave a small laugh. "Young, beautiful women are not that rare here. But it is said you are a woman of property. A business woman! Imagine! Here, we women are not allowed to think for ourselves. So you can understand how we envy and admire you. And each of us secretly hopes that you will be very successful, so you may pave the way for other women."

"I intend to succeed, Doña Yturria."

"I have no doubt of that," a voice said from behind Victoria. "Will you present me, Teresa?"

Victoria turned to find the businessman who had watched her so closely that day in the restaurant.

"Señora Garrett," Teresa Yturria said, with just a trace of speculation in her voice, "may I present the mayor of Brownsville, Matthew Farrington, Mayor Farrington, one of your citizens, Victoria Garrett."

"A loyal citizen, I hope," he said, bending over her hand.

"I hope so, Mayor Farrington," she murmured.

The man had a forceful, extremely male countenance and, although not handsome due to the crooked, flat nose, his smile conveyed a powerful sexuality. Noticing the silvering at the temples, Victoria judged him to be in his early forties.

"Have you had anything to eat yet?" he asked her.

"No, I haven't. But I'm waiting on my escort to finish his conversation with Don Yturria."

251

"Come along, Mrs. Garrett," he said, taking her elbow. "No lady should ever be forced to wait."

It was difficult for her to demur under his brusque, autocratic manner.

"Have you had a chance to meet any of the guests?" he asked.

"No, we only just arrived."

"Then there are some people here you should definitely be introduced to. For instance, Lew Wallace over there. He's governor-elect of the state of New Mexico. And Zachary Taylor, the one talking to Charles and Elizabeth Stillman. He's a rising politician."

They paused beneath the fronds of a date palm. Victoria pulled her shawl around her as the breeze from the sea cooled the balmy night air. "Mr. Farrington, why is it important I meet these people?"

"It's important to me," he said, taking her arm again and steering her toward the buffet table, "because I intend for you to be my wife, Mrs. Garrett."

"Your wife? Surely you're joking."

"Not in the least. Believe me, I'm quite serious."

"But you don't know anything about me, nor I you."

"On the contrary, I know all I need to know. How do you suppose you received an invitation to a party held by one of the most prominent families in Matamoros? I arranged it. Since I first noticed you in Pierre's, you've held my interest. And I must say you haven't disappointed me. When I learned you had outwitted Legs and Steve Kaptain for ownership of the *Corvette,* I was definitely intrigued. Your letter, which I received late yesterday, only confirmed my impression of your high intelligence."

"You've thoroughly explained what you know about me," she said, somewhat piqued to find her privacy had been invaded. "But, as I told you, I don't know anything about you."

"That is quickly remedied. By the end of my courtship, Victoria, I fully intend to have done away with any reluctance on your part."

XXIV

✠✠✠✠✠✠✠✠✠✠✠

Flowers arrived daily. Amanda, a young Negro girl Madame Gautier had procured for her, would bring the armful of gardenias, roses, or orchids into the parlor and hand her the card. The message was always the same: "I'm waiting for you to say yes. Matthew."

"I do declare, Mrs. Garrett," Amanda said, "this room looks like the inside of a greenhouse."

"And there's not room enough for one more vase, Amanda. Why don't you take some of the flowers home to your family this weekend."

"Aren't you going to that luncheon at Master Stillman's Saturday?"

"Yes, but I won't be needing you until Monday when I'm having the tea. Go ahead. And enjoy yourself."

Amanda left the room, delighted, and Victoria's thoughts turned to the Stillman luncheon and Matthew. Matthew was a forceful man, an aggressive one, and she knew he was gradually winning her. It was not the flowers, nor the small gifts. (Some of them were not that small. One was a beautiful opal necklace only recently mined in Guanajuato, which she sadly had to return, reminding Matthew it would be improper for her to accept the gift.)

It was the fact that she was coming to realize that Matthew and herself did make a good couple, complimenting one another. He had a dynamic personality, where she tried to be more reserved. And where there was an abrupt quality, a brusqueness, in his manner, her own sensitivity to others' feelings tended to soften his manner.

The fact that love had never been mentioned did not bother her. She knew she was cynical about the word, and, although Legs sometimes reproached her for her aloofness, she could see no room in her life for such a weakness as love.

That was not to say that Matthew did not care. In his own adoring way, he showered her with attention. The possessive way he held her elbow, the way he eagerly showed her off, told her he cared greatly.

The afternoon of the Stillman luncheon, his walnut-colored eyes never left her, although she was sure the people who tried to monopolize his time thought they were receiving his concentrated attention.

Victoria knew she could no longer delay her answer.

Matthew had been patient, unusual for him. But he wanted her and intended to have her. He told her as much outside the Stillman house. They had alighted from his private coach, and he had taken her hand, delaying her beneath the branches of a sycamore. She remembered thinking how the sun-dappled shadows softened the hardness of his countenance.

"Will you give me your answer, Victoria? Before we leave the party. I'm enormously proud of you and want everyone here today to know that you'll be mine."

It seemed to Victoria that everything was planned for Matthew . . . even her, as his showcase wife. But how could she condemn such a characteristic as wrong—when she, herself, had committed the same acts? Had not she planned for this very moment? When her name would be on the tip of every tongue, accepted by society, wealthy beyond care?

"I—I'll think about it, Matt."

"Good," he said, pressing her hand between his. "My sister and her husband are in town this week for the *Cinco de Mayo* fiestas. You'll meet them later this afternoon.

"By the way, dear, I've taken care of that problem you wrote me about. The young Mexican who complained to you his family had been cheated of their lands. His mother received a legal deed from Judge Haslett yesterday. The land around White Point is officially theirs."

It was at times like that Victoria wanted to hug Matthew. He could be extremely considerate. But she withheld her thanks as a corpulent Mexican woman admitted them inside.

They followed her to the parlor off the hall, where

the businessmen of Brownsville and their wives were gathered. A brown-skinned butler passed around drinks on a silver-plated tray. The clink of glasses and the hum of polite conversation filled the room.

Victoria took one glass, but Matthew declined, shaking his head.

"Why don't you drink, Matt?" she asked in a low voice.

"It hampers my ability to judge the moment. Besides," he said with a smooth smile, "I'm able to catch the indiscretions people make who do drink. These tidbits are often quite useful."

In this aspect, his cold-bloodness was chilling, but he did not give her time to dwell on it. "Come, dear," he said, propelling her into the crowd. "My banker looks like he's going to bust his money belt if he doesn't speak with me."

Victoria murmured the required exchanges to the banker and his wife, a dowdy, reticent woman, and tried to listen intently to the banker's monotonous monologue, wondering how such mundane things could possibly interest Matthew.

"I tell you, Matthew," the banker said, punctuating his words with a bony finger that jabbed the air, "it's an outrage when Mexican soldiers can capture American citizens. Why our men have no choice but to smuggle our merchandise across the border. It's either that or bribe those infernal duty inspectors."

His voice droned on, and Victoria lost interest—until Matthew replied, "General Brooke has already been informed. He's sent out two companies of Rangers under Kaptain to rescue them. But crossing the Mexican border is illegal. The government, of course, can't take any responsibility. It'll therefore, Howard, cost our merchants two grand—to pay the Rangers for their trouble."

Victoria heard the banker's breath suck in even as did her own. Steve was in Brownsville! Feelings, thoughts, and emotions whirled about her as if she were the eye of a hurricane.

But one thought dominated: Would Steve demand his payment—or, worse, would he betray her?

Almost spilling her drink, she set the glass down on a side table and excused herself from the banker's blusterous reply. She escaped through a door into the garden, where there was an old stable and carriage house. Nearby, in the shadows, was a welled cistern. It was to this she headed. Her heart thudded loudly as she sank in weakness on the well's rock-rimmed edge.

She had come so far—so far to lose everything in a moment! Surely Steve knew she was in Brownsville. There was no escape for her.

Her fist slammed against the well's rock. Why had she ever bought into the *Corvette*? Certainly it was a good investment, but there were other ventures just as profitable. She had been foolish in a weak moment. And now she would suffer the consequences of her act!

"Are you all right, Victoria?"

Victoria looked up to see Matthew there. "I'm sorry, Matt. I don't feel well. Perhaps it was the drink. Would you mind terribly if I went home?"

Matthew's probing eyes searched her face. "Not at all. Though my sister and her husband will be sorry they missed meeting you. I'll go make our excuses."

Dear Lord, what if he suspected something was amiss? He did not refer to her sudden sickness again, to Victoria's intense relief. But it was to his credit he never pried. To her dismay, Victoria never was placed in a position of defending her past, for not once did he question her about her life prior to her marriage to Ted.

By morning Victoria's panic had subsided. She had come to the conclusion that until she actually was confronted by Steve Kaptain, it was a situation with which she did not yet have to deal.

Meanwhile she planned to eliminate all ties that might link her to him. She was at her desk writing Belden a letter requesting he advertise her stock for sale in the next edition of the *Weekly Ranchero*, when Amanda admitted Matthew.

He pulled her from her chair before she could rise. "I refuse to wait, Victoria. And I refuse to let you say no."

"I believe perseverence is one of your best qualities, Matthew."

"I've made it a point in my life to concentrate on one problem at a time. And until you tell me yes, I will let nothing else in my life interfere."

Victoria pulled away slightly. "And if I say yes? Will I be set aside as a problem solved, while you continue to work on other problems?"

"You know me better than that. Even if I didn't love you, I'd never let you be unhappy. It'd be admitting defeat . . . and that I'll never submit to."

"But you do love me?"

He pulled her close, and she could sense passion rolling like rapids through his powerful body. "I fear, Victoria, you'll be my only weakness. Your spirit, your intelligence, your beauty—I have to have you," he whispered thickly against her hair.

"Then your answer is yes," she said, before his mouth closed possessively over hers.

Her sleep that night was troubled. She awoke, breathing heavily, as if the nameless dream had followed her even into reality. And then she knew why the nightmare still persisted. Someone was in the room with her.

"Who's there?" she asked tremulously of the dark.

A tiny flame appeared as a match was struck. Steve bent to light the kerosene lamp on the table, his face Satanically handsome above the flame of the match.

"How did you get in here?" she demanded.

"It wasn't difficult." He shook out the match, eyeing her tumbled hair and blazing eyes, before his gaze dropped to the rumpled beige flannel gown with its ribbons tied at her throat and wrists. "Just got in from Mexico."

She drew a deep breath. "All right, Steve. What is it you want?"

He sat on the bed facing her, his back propped against one of the four posts and one dusty boot resting on the coverlet.

"I want to know why the hell you bought into the *Corvette*."

She had been dreading that question, knowing he would ask it, knowing he would not let her off easy. Several times she had stood before her mirror practicing an answer.

"Well, I—I felt it would be a good investment. Besides," she said, now defensive, as he raised a skeptical brow, "why shouldn't I? It's my money. You don't own me, Steve Kaptain, and you'd better get—"

He grabbed the hand she shook at him denouncingly and jerked her to him so that she sprawled across the bed on her stomach. With a shove, he rolled her over and lay across her rib cage so that she was pinned beneath him. Her wrists he held stretched above her head with one hand. A handful of her heavy hair he savagely tangled with the other, so that her slim neck was arched backwards in the graceful line of a swan's. Her blue eyes, smoky with pain—and something else—were forced to look up into his face through the thick layers of her sooty lashes.

"Damn it, Vicky! When will you get it through that stubborn head of yours what you're running from?"

"I—I don't know what you mean," she whispered in gasps.

"Then I'll tell you." His dark green eyes looked through her with cool determination, as if he wished to reach some secret place within her soul. "You're running from yourself. Oh, you can play society's grand lady and fool them into believing your subdued respectability. But you, yourself, will know it's a facade. And you'll be as restless as a wild horse corralled."

His voice sank to a husky whisper. "And when you accept what I say as the truth, you'll realize it's only with me, *corazón*, you can be your real self—headstrong, wild, passionate."

He released her wrists but did not rise from her. For a long moment their gazes locked, their wills pitted in silent struggle. Intensely aware of him with every separate cell in her body, Victoria capitulated, raising her arms to wrap about the muscled column of his neck.

"Damn your black soul!" she whispered.

As Steve lowered his mouth on her, he saw her passion mutate the brilliant blue of her eyes to a dusky purple. Damn it, would he never get the wanting of her out of his system? Would he ever understand her? At one moment she was a young girl, full of charming naïveté and surprisingly vulnerable; at the next moment she was a determined woman with a sharp wit and a tongue to match. At one moment she was cursing him with every breath she drew, and the next loving him with a passion as deep and strong as his own.

In that moment of complete submission, Victoria knew the rapturous sensation experienced by few women. A pleasant warmth spread through her, building to such an intensity that it seemed her very blood boiled with desire for Steve. Her body thrilled at the touch of his brown hands, raising her passions to a height she found unbearable to sustain.

Yet even as he yanked loose the yellow ribbon tied at her throat, even as she ripped at the buttons of his faded blue shirt, she drew back, her breasts heaving with desire that went unfulfilled.

Steve raised on one arm. His long, narrowed eyes asked the question the tight lips did not. A taut restraint separated them though their bodies still clung.

"Steve, I can't. I'm to marry Matthew Farrington. In two months." Trembling, she waited for his reaction, her eyes pleading for understanding.

For what seemed like eternity, the reaction did not come. Then, as easily as the mountain cat, he rolled to his feet, so that he stood above her. One hand rested on the bed's post.

"*Corazón*, you once accused me of being an opportunist, of being mercenary. I think you'd better take a close look at that honor you hold so damned high, before you make any more accusations."

He turned to leave, and she said, "What are you going to do?"

He looked around at her, his face harsh with suppressed anger. "Right now I'm going to find me a woman, Vicky. A real woman. Not some machine!"

XXV

✢✢✢✢✢✢✢✢✢✢✢✢

Scarcely less than three weeks had passed, when Victoria stood on the lower steps of the rosewood staircase and watched the people stream through the open double doors of Matthew's palatial home, which was said to rival the Stillman house.

The scene reminded her of another time . . . another engagement ball. But then she had been the housekeeper. Now, within a month, she would be the mistress.

Matthew took her hand proudly, placing a light kiss just above the large blue-diamond engagement ring. "You've made me enormously happy, Victoria. And I want every person in Brownsville tonight to share my happiness. This will be the biggest event of the year—second only to our wedding."

Victoria was humbled by his sincere pleasure and was determined to be the kind of wife he wanted. She smiled and tried to find something personal to say to each guest they greeted, though she found, to her dismay, society's polished conversation superficial. Would the boring evening never end?

Only Legs, his dejection hidden from view by his poker face, cast a shadow on the ball. For his friendship meant a lot to Victoria, and she suspected he did not entirely approve of her betrothal to Matthew. Still, he took her hand warmly, wishing her the best, before shaking hands with Matthew.

A real moment of pleasure came when Dick King introduced Victoria to his wife, Henrietta, a solemn, plain young woman with intelligent hazel eyes.

"You be a lucky man, Matthew Farrington, to have such a bonny colleen. My Etta told me you be needing someone like Mrs. Garrett here."

Blushing, Victoria had meant only to give Matthew's hand an affectionate squeeze. But it tightened into a child's grip of fear. Matthew looked at her with a frown of concern.

"What is it?"

"Nothing. Just—just someone I thought I recognized."

But she knew it had to be him. No other man was that tall—with that peculiar shade of mahogany-colored hair curling at the nape of his neck. Then he looked around, and penetrating sage green eyes surrounded by the forest of lashes met hers.

Dear God, would she never escape him? Would both her body and spirit be his forever, to play with one moment and torture the next?

Her blood congealed as he slowly made his way through the packed room to the foot of the staircase, his eyes never once releasing her from the agony she suffered.

Henrietta recognized him and said, "Mr. Kaptain! How nice to see you again. Dick and I enjoyed your company so much at our home last year."

Victoria could not hear Steve's low reply, but she saw Henrietta smile warmly and was infuriated at the considerate attention Steve gave some women while his treatment of her was so dispassionate, so cursory and careless. Henrietta seemed to blossom under Steve's natural courtesy, and Victoria suddenly found she disliked the woman.

Steve wore a black frock coat over a white linen shirt with frilled cuffs and collar and a black embroidered vest. All he needed was a ring in one ear, Victoria thought scathingly, and he would look just like a pirate. But he did look diabolically handsome. No, not handsome. He would never be handsome. The face was too scarred, too browned, too rough-cast. But . . . But striking in a rugged, masculine, and—yes, irresistible way.

"Matthew," Dick said, "I be pleased to introduce you to a friend of Etta's and mine, Steve Kaptain. Steve, our mayor, Matthew Farrington."

Standing as he was on the bottom stair, Steve still towered above her while his steady gaze was on a level with Matthew's eyes. "May I offer my congratulations,

Mayor Farrington. And my best wishes to your fiancée."

His eyes flicked over her carelessly. The *bastard*! He found it amusing to see her squirm, to see her writhe in apprehension. Her square chin lifted, and her blue eyes blazed at the laughing green ones.

The two men shook hands, and Matthew said, "You are the scout I believe General Brooke recommended to lead the Rangers into Mexico last month. I heard you did a remarkable job."

Steve smiled wryly. "The two thousand your generous citizens offered made the expedition well worth the danger."

Dick laughed, his loud voice booming in the large room. "We be hearing your men brought back more than just the Americans and their goods, Steve. Rumor says you brought back the shirts and pants of the thirty-seven Mexican soldiers who captured the Americans."

The people gathered there at the foot of the stairs joined in the laughter—all but Victoria—and Steve replied lightly, "It went something like that."

When the laughter had ebbed, Matthew said, "Ford tells me you were posted some time ago in San Antonio. Perhaps you knew my sister, Alice? Alice Farrington?"

"Yes," Steve said, his gaze resting lightly on Victoria. His long lips curled at the ends. "I had the pleasure of meeting Alice several times. I believe she married Enrique Silva."

Victoria was struck dumb—as if paralyzed by a bolt of lightning. Alice Farrington! Why had she never made the connection? More than once, Victoria remembered, Alice had mentioned, in that supercilious way she had, of having a brother who was a mayor.

"Then I'm sure," Matthew said, "Alice will be delighted to learn you're here. She and Enrique should arrive a little later. My sister has never been one for punctuality.

"Darling," Matthew said, turning to Victoria, "I see Judge Haslett there motioning for my attention. Will you excuse me for a moment?"

He turned back to Steve. "Perhaps, Mr. Kaptain, you'll be kind enough to entertain my fiancée for a moment. I believe the musicians are beginning to play again. I'm sure you would like to dance, wouldn't you, darling?"

Victoria nodded mutely, and Steve said, "It would be an honor."

Matthew departed with his usual brusqueness, and, like a sleepwalker, Victoria allowed Steve to lead her into the ballroom. He took her firmly by the waist and swept her into the midst of the other dancing couples.

Neither of them spoke to break the tension. Victoria finally managed to look up into that swarthy face. The green eyes swept over her wickedly. She knew he held all the aces.

"So you've won," she said wearily, feeling the fight fade from her. "Enrique and Alice will back up any accusations you make to Matt."

"You're wrong, *corazón*. Neither of them will ever speak a word of what happened in San Antonio."

"Maybe not Enrique," she said sarcastically. "He wouldn't want to take the chance of his love affair with another man being exposed. But Alice would. She dislikes me intensely."

"I doubt it. Alice is just as afraid of being discovered."

"What do you mean?"

"It appears her husband is so busy with Pedro, he can't satisfy his wife. So it seems she's taking lovers."

"How do you know all this?"

Steve smiled. "I just left her bed."

"Oh! Oh!" Victoria halted in the midst of the dancing, stamping her foot in outrage. "And you have the arrogance to come here tonight—with the smell of that—of her all over you!"

She tried to withdraw from Steve's embrace, but he laughed and held her tighter. "Uh-uh, Vicky. Remember, the eyes of Brownsville society are upon you." His hand about her waist forced her to move again into the steps of the waltz.

There was a wooden smile on her lips. "Then what is it that you want, Steve Kaptain?"

"Don't freeze up, Vicky. Your secrets are safe with me."

She looked at him witheringly. "I don't believe you. You're not to be trusted."

He shrugged. "You were willing enough to entrust your precious life to me back there in San Antonio. However, you have no need to fear me. You see, Vicky, since you've sold yourself to the highest bidder, I somehow find your payment not worth collecting."

Momentarily she stumbled over the steps of the dance. Steve always had a way of breaking her with his cutting words. Yet she would never let him have the satisfaction of seeing the pain he inflicted. She pulled herself up straight.

"Then why are you here tonight?" she demanded,

her blue eyes as dark as stormy seas and flashing all the hate she had ever felt for him.

Steve probed her face intently, looking for what, she did not know. "I did some soul-searching—after I left your place that night. I knew that I was partly responsible for all that had happened between us."

"And you came here just to make your apologies?" she asked, her voice caustic.

"Nope. When I found out Alice was in town, I figured I'd pay her a visit. Persuade her"—he flashed Victoria a mocking grin—"to put away her dislike for you. Sort of my way of settling accounts between you and me."

"I see."

"Nope, Vicky. You'll never see. You're too headstrong, too distrustful, and—too ambitious."

The music came to an end, and Steve bowed elaborately. "Madam, my best to you. Good-bye."

XXVI

✻✻✻✻✻✻✻✻✻✻

"Turn slowly, *chérie.*"

Victoria did as Madame Gautier bade. On her knees, the French woman stuck the remaining pins in the hem of Victoria's gown.

"Ahhh, *ma petite,*" she said, rising and clasping her hands in delight, "you are enchanting. My creation is a masterpiece. Your wedding dress will be discussed for months after the wedding!"

Victoria turned and looked in the full-length mirror. Madame Gautier was telling the truth, she knew. The white satin fell from its empire cut, below her high-thrust breast, tapering in the long train that swirled about white kid slippers. The long lace sleeves, tapering to a point just below her wrists, matched the veil supported by a tiara of pearls. Madame Gautier had pulled her hair, startling black against all the white, up through the ring of the tiara and over the back so that the curls fell in a cascade of ringlets about the upper half of the veil.

"You are simply stunning!" she repeated.

Victoria reached up and unpinned the tiara. "You've done a marvelous job, Madame. When will the dress be ready?"

"By the end of the month. In time for your wedding. I promise."

"Good. I'll send Amanda by for it. Now I must get out of this before Matthew arrives."

"Oui, it is most unlucky to be seen in your wedding dress before the wedding, is it not, *chérie?"*

It was a rhetorical question, but Victoria was tempted to tell her she no longer feared bad luck. It seemed to her that she had faced everything and had survived.

The night of her engagement ball she had endured Enrique's toadying, Alice's simpering, and, worst of all, Steve's mockery. It had been a tempering point, when one either breaks or passes through the fire stronger, more resilient. And yet, she felt no triumph.

"Monsieur's coach is here," Madame Gautier said, as she passed Victoria's dress behind the carved wooden screen to her.

Matthew was charged with enthusiasm. "Darling," he said, handing her into the carriage and seating himself beside her, "Governor Bell has telegraphed his acceptance of our wedding invitation. I don't need to tell you what this means. The influence it'll have on my career. The goals I've plotted for Brownsville can now be achieved."

Victoria put her hand over his. "I'm so happy for you, Matt. Your reelection is assured with his backing, isn't it?"

Matthew looked at her appreciatively. Her intelligent grasp of situations, her support, and that warm beauty that hid the blazing fires of passion that, he was sure, lay just beneath the surface—they were all he had hoped to find in a woman.

"Without a doubt," he answered. "And after two terms as mayor"—he spread his hands expansively—"there is no limit to how high we can climb together."

"Matt, can we drive down along the riverfront before you take me home?"

"Why, of course, darling. I'm proud to show you off."

The riverfront was one of her favorite places. The palm-arched drive that paralleled the Rio Grande, the sight of the steamboats—their paddle wheels splashing harmoniously in the water, the little Mexican *aquaderos* trudging along behind oxcarts loaded with water barrels, and the wharves piled with tobacco and coffee and hides. The excitement. Brownsville's drawing rooms held nothing in comparison.

Matthew pulled the carriage off onto the rutted road that, leaving the bustling town behind it, wound its way alongside the river. Shading the carriage's two occupants from the near-tropical sun were the Spanish live oaks, with their long, gloomy-looking moss hanging like mourning crepe.

The carriage came to a brake of sugar cane, and

Matthew edged the rig off onto the soft shoulder of the dirt road. "All right, Victoria," he said quietly, putting his arm on the seat behind her. "I know there is something you have to say."

That was one thing Victoria admired about Matthew. He was direct and did not waste time with meaningless chatter. But, dear Lord, his directness made it so much harder for her to tell him.

"Matt, I've—I've changed my mind."

"I suspected that."

He seemed calm, and she rushed on to explain herself. "Oh, Matt, I like you very much. But my idea of marriage—well, it's not the same as yours. I don't like being paraded as one of your trophies."

"And do you think that's how I feel?"

"I don't think you know you feel that way. And it's not your fault. You've been brought up in that kind of background. The idea that everything—even marriage and love—must serve a purpose in your life. And I don't think you can dictate love, Matt."

She put one hand over her eyes. "I don't think I'm making myself clear. I don't even understand it fully myself. I may be making the biggest mistake of my life. I've waited almost all my life for this very moment"—she looked up directly in his eyes, her own filled with tears—"but I know, Matt, this wasn't what I wanted."

"I don't think you know what you really want."

"Maybe I don't," she cried out, "but I know what I don't want. And it's a plotted marriage—like your plotted city!"

Matthew's voice was calm. "Victoria, I love you.

And I'll make any necessary changes in my life to give you happiness."

"Oh, Matt! It's not all your fault. I'm not being fair to you, either. In my own way, although I've called it a love of sorts, I've used you also. I've used you as the quickest road to acceptance and security. Matt, you deserve more than just a parasitic wife."

"I don't want a parasitic wife, Victoria. I want you."

"You don't know anything about me! That I worked in a bordello, that I've been involved in a murder, that—"

He placed blunt fingertips on her lips. "You don't have to continue. I've known all that for a long time."

"How could you know."

"You don't think I'd ask you to be my wife unless I knew everything about you? There would always be the chance of blackmail hurting us. And you know by now I never leave anything to chance."

"You knew about Steve?"

"Of course. That's why I had the expedition offered to him. I wanted to confront you two with each other for a final time."

"You didn't need to. There was never anything but hate between Steve and myself."

"I know that now."

"Then you also know that there's no true love between you and myself, Matt. Whatever security, whatever acceptance I finally find, I'll do it on my own."

Matthew kissed her lightly on the lips and brushed away a tear from her cheeks. "I know that also, Victoria. And I'm too cocky to humble myself by begging you."

"Will you take me back to town, then?"

As Matthew drove the carriage back into Brownsville, a breeze blew up the river from the sea, bringing
relief from the summer heat. But no relief from the
desolation that, like a glacier, slowly chilled every
nerve in Victoria's body.

XXVII

✺✺✺✺✺✺✺✺✺✺✺

Amanda, her head bound in a turbanlike cloth, lit the candles. Their flickering light drove the shadows from the room. "Lord, Mrs. Garrett, I didn't know you was still sitting here."

Victoria blinked, unaccustomed to the light. "What time is it, Amanda?"

"Going on ten, Mrs. Garrett."

There was still time—if Legs was in. "Amanda, have the carriage brought around front."

She hurried to her bedroom and changed into the green gabardine that was one of her favorites. It had a heavy capelike bodice that would protect her against

Brownsville's night air, which could carry a slight chill with its saltiness. Oh God, what if he no longer wanted her? She took one last look in the mirror, afraid to find she had outwardly changed. But although the creamy complexion had been altered by the sun to honey gold, the light blue eyes were still as brilliant, the full, pink lips just as soft and inviting. She tucked the stray curls that had escaped to tumble about her shoulders back in place before hurrying to the waiting carriage.

The horse clip-clopped through the brick-laid streets, its shoes echoing ghostly in the night. Distractedly, she urged her driver faster. Her heart pounded as she raised the knocker to the small set of apartments belonging to Legs. What if he did not answer?

Legs opened the door himself. "Victoria," he said, taking the cigar from his lips in surprise. "Don't tell me. You've broken your engagement with Matthew."

She laughed at the roguish smile on his face. "Yes. Three days ago. Were you so certain it would happen?"

"Any fool could see he wasn't for you. Now come in out of the dark."

"No, I can't, Legs. I need your help. Can you come with me? Now?"

He took her hand and helped her back into the carriage. "What is it?" he asked, looking up at her.

She hated raising his hopes and then disappointing him, but she was a woman tormented. "Legs, I have to find Steve . . . if he's still in town."

"Oh?" His eyes were half closed in that way he had of appraising a situation.

For a minute her breath held. She could not blame him if he were to refuse her.

He shrugged. "I always knew I'd lose to Steve. Damned best poker player this side of Matamoros."

"Then you'll help me?"

"I have a good idea where he is—probably in one of those *fandango* houses across the border playing monte. If you're serious about looking for him, wrap that shawl about your face."

Twenty minutes later they were in the squalid part of Matamoros. Several groups of Mexicans stood around the lantern-lit corners, dressed in the picturesque native garb—brightly colored woolen blankets wrapped around them and broad-brimmed sombreros on their heads. Sometimes an American was to be found among them, south of the border for a good time at one of the dancing amusements.

The strains of a fiddle brought Victoria and Legs to a building on the square near the church. Afraid to leave her alone in the carriage, Legs took her with him, making her promise to hide her face beneath the shawl.

They entered a long, narrow room where, fastened on the wall, two or three wax candles dimly burned. A number of young women, dressed in their best finery, sat on benches at the end of the room, waiting for an invitation to dance.

However, they were little noticed at the time by the men present, as were the musicians who, without interruption, played the same monotonous piece of dance music time after time.

At the other end of the room stood a few tables at which games of chance were being played. A motley mixture of Mexicans and Americans crowded around these tables.

"They're playing monte," Legs explained in a whisper. "The Mexican is passionately addicted to it."

Piles of Spanish dollars and gold pieces were heaped upon the tables, in noticeable contrast to the wretched state of the place and the shabby dress of the Mexicans. At one table an old Mexican woman was banker.

Now and then the play was interrupted as some of the observers and a few of the players, usually Americans, decided to dance. Victoria noticed that some of the women who waited patiently for a partner were beautiful, with fiery black eyes and comely figures.

In the near-darkness it was almost impossible for her to distinguish one man from another. "Do you see him, Legs?" she asked in a whisper.

Legs shook his head. "We'll try another place."

After visiting several more public dance halls, she came to realize that the places were all the same. The rooms in which the gambling took place, the gambling tables, the black-eyed señoritas. She also noted that only the Mexican women of poorer families visited the *fandangos*.

Toward midnight she and Legs had about given up their search, when she noticed a large Appaloosa tied to a railing outside another sleazy-looking building from which issued *fandango* music.

"Legs, let's try this one. Just one more. I know Steve's in there. That's his horse, I'm sure."

Legs sighed. "All right. But this is the last one. It gets damned dangerous around here after midnight. I don't fancy having my throat slit—nor yours—in defense of your beautiful face, my lovely."

She smiled at his attempted jocularity. "Legs, you're marvelous!"

"But that doesn't make you want me any the more, does it? Now hush, and cover your face."

They entered the dimly lit room and began to make their way toward the gambling tables. Dear Lord, she prayed silently, don't let me find Steve in some back room with one of the flashing-eyed maidens.

She need not have worried. Steve was sitting at the first table they came to, arrogantly chewing on a cigar as the pile before him grew. For a moment she merely watched, her eyes roaming hungrily over his face.

In less than the breadth of a second pictures of that face flashed through her mind—Steve massaging her frostbitten feet, Steve studying her across the flames of a flickering campfire, Steve cradling a wet Jason in his arms. Steve raping and making love to her all in one violent and passion-filled moment.

She knew then why she had feared him so. Why she had fought him so long. It had not been he she was fighting, but herself. He had been right that evening he had come to her house. He had been right all along. It was herself she had been fighting. She was fighting the love for him that possessed her, that bound her to him.

She turned to Legs, but he had gone. Instead, she reached in her reticule and pulled out one of the gold pieces she now carried. She tossed it in the center of the table.

The gold coin clinked among the others, and Steve looked up. For a moment, she did not think he recognized her. Then, one black brow lifted in amusement, and his white teeth gleamed in the darkness.

Slowly, inexorably, he rose from the chair, shoving his winnings back into the table's center. There were some yelps of pleasure as he left the table and crossed the distance that separated the two of them.

"It took you long enough," he said, removing the shawl from her face.

Had she not said the same of him once, when he had come looking for her?

"You knew I'd find out?" she asked quietly.

"That you loved me? Nope, you're too unpredictable, *corazón*. I could only wait and hope."

"Steve, let's go. I'm homesick for Sierra Diablo."

He kissed her then, gently, tenderly, even as the customers cheered and shouted ribald phrases.

ALL TIME BESTSELLERS
FROM POPULAR LIBRARY

☐	THE BERLIN CONNECTION—Simmel	08607-6	1.95
☐	THE BEST PEOPLE—Van Slyke	08456-1	1.75
☐	A BRIDGE TOO FAR—Ryan	08373-5	2.50
☐	THE CAESAR CODE—Simmel	08413-8	1.95
☐	DO BLACK PATENT LEATHER SHOES REALLY REFLECT UP?—Powers	08490-1	1.75
☐	ELIZABETH—Hamilton	04013-0	1.75
☐	THE FURY—Farris	08620-3	2.25
☐	THE HAB THEORY—Eckerty	08597-5	2.50
☐	HARDACRE—Skelton	04026-2	2.25
☐	THE HEART LISTENS—Van Slyke	08520-7	1.95
☐	TO KILL A MOCKINGBIRD—Lee	08376-X	1.50
☐	THE LAST BATTLE—Ryan	08381-6	2.25
☐	THE LAST CATHOLIC IN AMERICA—Powers	08528-2	1.50
☐	THE LONGEST DAY—Ryan	08380-8	1.95
☐	LOVE'S WILD DESIRE—Blake	08616-5	1.95
☐	THE MIXED BLESSING—Van Slyke	08491-X	1.95
☐	MORWENNA—Goring	08604-1	1.95
☐	THE RICH AND THE RIGHTEOUS —Van Slyke	08585-1	1.95

Buy them at your local bookstores or use this handy coupon for ordering:

B-17

Popular Library, P.O. Box 5755, Terre Haute, Indiana 47805

Please send me the books I have checked above. Orders for less than 5 books must include 60c for the first book and 25c for each additional book to cover mailing and handling. Orders of 5 or more books postage is Free. I enclose $_____ in check or money order.

Name_____

Address_____

City_____ State/Zip_____

Please allow 4 to 5 weeks for delivery. This offer expires 6/78.

Dorothy Dunnett
THE LYMOND CHRONICLE

THE GREATEST HISTORICAL SAGA OF OUR AGE BY A WRITER "AS GOOD AS MARY RENAULT" (*Sunday Times*, London), "AS POPULAR AS TOLKIEN" (Cleveland Magazine), WHO "COULD TEACH SCHEHERAZADE A THING OR TWO ABOUT SUSPENSE, PACE AND INVENTION" (*New York Times*), AND WHO IS "ONE OF THE GREATEST TALE-SPINNERS SINCE DUMAS" (*Cleveland Plain Dealer*).